Kayla Morgan. Dustin's new doctor.

She made him want things more in keeping with the old Tom Jamieson. The live hard, play hard party animal. The man he'd been before a bullet had stopped him in his tracks a little over two years ago. His near-death experience had forced him to reassess his priorities. Made him realise he wanted to go home to his roots, build his future there.

Start a family.

To do that he needed a wife, and he knew what he was looking for. A down-to-earth woman, someone loving and generous. Someone with a sense of humour.

Not someone like Kayla. She was a city girl through and through. Polished perfection, dressed to the nines, designer labels, never a hair out of place. Positively stingy with her smiles.

Cool, reserved, fastidious.

For all that his brain knew what he *needed,* his body *wanted* otherwise. Kayla made him want to howl, beat his chest, risk potential frostbite to get close to her. He didn't much like this glimpse of his old self. That harder, hungrier, edgier man who wanted nothing more than to get Kayla Morgan into his bed…

Born in New Zealand, **Sharon Archer** now lives in County Victoria, Australia, with her husband Glenn, one lame horse and five pensionable hens. Always an avid reader, she discovered Mills & Boon as a teenager through Lucy Walker's fabulous Outback Australia stories. Now she lives in a gorgeous bush setting, and loves the native fauna that visits regularly... Well, maybe not the possum which coughs outside the bedroom window in the middle of the night.

The move to acreage brought a keen interest in bushfire management (she runs the fireguard group in her area), as well as free time to dabble in woodwork, genealogy (her advice is...don't get her started!), horse-riding and motorcycling—as a pillion or in charge of the handlebars.

Free time turned into words on paper! And the dream to be a writer gathered momentum. With her background in a medical laboratory, what better line to write for than Mills & Boon® Medical™ Romance?

Recent titles by the same author:

BACHELOR DAD, GIRL-NEXT-DOOR
MARRIAGE REUNITED, BABY ON THE WAY
SINGLE FATHER: WIFE AND MOTHER WANTED

THE MAN
BEHIND THE BADGE

BY
SHARON ARCHER

First published in Great Britain 2011
by Mills & Boon, an imprint of Harlequin (UK) Limited,
Eton House, 18-24 Paradise Road, Richmond, Surrey TW9 1SR

© Sharon Archer 2011

ISBN: 978 0 263 21898 5

Harlequin (UK) policy is to use papers that are natural,
renewable and recyclable products and made from wood grown in
sustainable forests. The logging and manufacturing process conform
to the legal environmental regulations of the country of origin.

Printed and bound in Great Britain
by CPI Antony Rowe, Chippenham, Wiltshire

THE MAN
BEHIND THE BADGE

My thanks to lovely friends Anna Campbell
and Nikki Logan, and especially Rachel Bailey,
for listening and for the chance to bounce around ideas.

And always my thanks to Glenn!

CHAPTER ONE

TOM JAMIESON reached into the cabin of his four-wheel drive and slotted the handpiece of the police radio back into its cradle. He straightened, stripped off the yellow reflective safety vest and tossed it on the passenger's seat. The perspiration that had made his black T-shirt cling had begun to cool. Flexing his tired shoulders, he ran a hand over his face and felt the stubble rasp across his palm. It had been a long day and a longer evening but, for all the frustration, it had been oddly satisfying.

He smiled wryly as he listened to frogs croaking in a distant chorus. His city colleagues wouldn't believe the action that made up his average working tasks these days.

He breathed in a deep lungful of fragrant eucalyptus, the clean tangy oils still heavy in the air after a hot day. In the nearby trees, a lone magpie chortled, its diurnal senses confused by the brightness of the full moon. The gentle night sounds and scents gathered around him like a cloak of serenity.

Coming back to Dustin had been the right choice for him.

In the paddock beside him, a dozen bovine silhouettes munched contentedly on the pasture in their temporary new home. Moonlight gleamed off the black hides of the now-sedate Angus yearlings. A far cry from the fractious cavorters that had led him and his helpers on an hour-long chase along the roadside.

He shifted, reaching for the vehicle door. Time to go home, get out of clothes that carried the aroma of cowpats and get clean. His stomach growled.

Shower. Food. Sleep. In that order.

A set of approaching headlights stabbed the night to form a weird hazy glow in a patch of low-lying mist. Tom glanced at the clock on the dashboard. Nearly one in the morning. An odd time to be travelling into Dustin on a Sunday night. He watched with reluctant curiosity as the car drew nearer.

A few seconds later, he recognised the shape of the small car. He frowned as his heart thumped hard.

Kayla Morgan.

Dustin's new doctor.

And currently the woman he fancied more than common sense dictated—especially given that she barely acknowledged his existence.

As the car zipped across the end of the side road where he was parked, Kayla's pale face was illuminated briefly in the side window. She glanced his way and for a second her eyes seemed to look right at him. His hand lifted in an automatic salute even though he doubted that she'd looked long enough to see him let alone identify him. Pretty much par for the course with their social interaction to date. He huffed out a self-mocking snort.

He, on the other hand, noticed every minuscule detail about her. From the top of her honey-blonde head to the cheeky pink-tinted toenails that peeped out of the sandals she'd worn to the hospital barbecue when she'd first arrived in town two months ago. Even her eye colour...he'd never been fanciful about eye colour. Irises were blue, brown, green, hazel— standard cop's vocabulary. But not when it came to Kayla. Nope. She looked straight through him with eyes the colour of polished pewter.

She made him want things more in keeping with the old Tom Jamieson. The live-hard, play-hard party animal. The man he'd been before a bullet had stopped him in his tracks a little over two years ago. His near-death experience, the time in hospital and then the months of rehabilitation afterwards had forced him to reassess his priorities. Made him realise he wanted to go home to his roots, build his future there.

Start a family.

To do that he needed a wife and he knew what he was looking for. A down-to-earth woman, someone loving and generous. Someone with a sense of humour.

Not someone like Kayla. She was a city girl through and through. Polished perfection, dressed to the nines, designer labels, never a hair out of place. Positively stingy with her smiles.

Cool, reserved, fastidious.

For all that his brain knew what he *needed*, his body *wanted* otherwise. Kayla made him want to howl, beat his chest, risk potential frostbite to get close to her. He didn't much like this glimpse of his old self. That harder, hungrier, edgier man who wanted nothing more than to get Kayla Morgan into his bed…even when she flicked her unusual silver eyes over him as though he was invisible.

He frowned as he yanked open the car door and slid behind the wheel. What the hell was she doing in Dustin anyway, besides upsetting his equilibrium? He knew the short answer. She was working at the hospital and ultimately filling in as a medical locum for Liz Campbell's maternity leave.

But what had made her want to come all the way out here, to his country town, when she so obviously didn't belong?

And now she was returning after another weekend in the big smoke. Had she been getting a fix of civilisation, something to sustain her for her sentence in rural purgatory? Or did she have a man tucked away down there?

Someone happy to have a long-distance relationship with her?

Someone as controlled and contained as she was?

An image leapt into his mind. Male hands other than his touching her, sliding over that perfect, creamy skin. He cursed under his breath.

Jaw set tight, he slammed the vehicle door. The fangs of unrequited lust sank deep. He was slowly going crazy.

After clipping the seat belt, he reached for the ignition key.

An unholy shriek of brakes sliced through the air, the brutal noise cutting off the gentle murmurs of the mellow night. For a split second, Tom froze. Then, pulse rocketing, he jerked his head towards the sound. In the distance, a strange light show played erratically across the vegetation. Yellow beams dipped and spun like out-of-control searchlights. A moment later, everything stopped with a sickening crunch of metal.

Kayla!

A shaft of icy dread pierced his gut. With a quick, hard rev of the engine, he accelerated down the short stretch of gravel road to the intersection and spun the steering-wheel in the direction of the now stationary lights. His vehicle leapt forward as the tyres gripped the sealed road.

God, what would he find? The thought of that feminine perfection injured—or worse—appalled him.

His low beam cut through the thickening wisps of pale fog. The small jelly-bean-pink car was sitting diagonally across the middle of the road. It looked whole but perhaps the damage was on the other side.

On the driver's side.

He was still too far away to see clearly inside the vehicle, to see if there was any movement. He leaned forward over his steering-wheel, as though that would somehow help his vision.

A moment later, her car moved, headlights swinging around in a U-turn.

He swallowed, shaken by an abrupt wash of relief that left his joints momentarily water weak.

Kayla was all right, the car was whole.

Her headlights kept moving and for the first time Tom noticed a dark blue sedan with its bonnet crumpled against the trunk of a gum tree.

Her car stopped with the beam of lights trained on the wreck.

He positioned his vehicle across the lane to block any on-coming traffic, emergency lights flashing and his headlights adding to the brightness of Kayla's. Her door opened and she scrambled out. He yanked on his handbrake and uttered a pithy curse as she ran towards the wreck.

What was the woman doing? The scene needed to be se-cured before she went charging in. They'd had no rain for weeks. Fire danger at the moment was extreme. Hot exhaust, long grass. A recipe for disaster.

As Tom threw open his door, a man's guttural cries echoed in his ears.

'Help me! Somebody. Please. Please.'

Fire extinguisher, woollen blanket and torch in hand, Tom ran to the front of the crumpled bonnet. The sweetly nauseat-ing tang of petrol fumes filled his sinuses. In his peripheral vision, he was aware of Kayla swinging the driver's door wide.

'It's all right, we'll look after you,' she said, loudly enough to cut through the man's groans. She sounded firm, confident. Trustworthy. 'What's your name?'

'A-Andy.'

Charred grass smouldered and, even as Tom scuffed dirt into the blackening area, a flame flickered to life in the dry leaf litter around the trunk of the tree. Crisp twigs crunched beneath his boot as he stamped out the fledgling fire. He spread the blanket strategically to smother the tinder dry fuel.

'Hello, Andy. My name's Kayla. I'm a doctor.'

With one ear on Kayla's conversation, Tom shone his torch into the engine cavity beneath the buckled bonnet. No obvious hot spots or smoke at this stage but that could change in an instant.

'You're going to be fine.' Her soothing voice continued. 'We'll look after you now.'

Tom placed the extinguisher on the ground within easy access then strode to where Kayla was crouched at the open driver's door. She'd positioned a cervical collar around the victim's neck and was shining a small pencil-slim torchlight into the man's eyes.

Tom leaned low and growled at her, 'This scene is not safe.'

'Then please organise it for us, Sergeant.' She sounded pleasant but remote. Her attention was fixed on her patient and she didn't look up.

Tom smiled grimly as he braced his hand on the top of the door and reached across her towards the steering column. At least she knew who he was. 'I have organised it, *Doctor.*'

'Well done.' The casual, dismissive praise rankled as he watched her twist further into the car and dig her hands down either side of the man in front of her. 'Any pain anywhere, Andy?'

'M-my ankle.' The slurred words were accompanied by a belch of stale alcohol. Tom could smell it even though he wasn't directly in its path. Kayla didn't flinch.

'Okay, I'll have a look.'

Tom gritted his teeth as his fingers found the key in the ignition. It was in the off position. 'We need to get Andy out. *Now.* There's—' His train of thought dried up abruptly as Kayla shifted to the right and the bare skin on her shoulder brushed the sensitive skin of his inner arm. Electricity sizzled along his nerves, making his fingers fumble with the car key. He forced his thoughts back into line. 'Kayla, there's petrol vapour, a hot exhaust, tinder-dry grass. The danger of fire is extreme.'

She glanced around at him then and gave a quick, short nod. 'Of course. I understand. We need to move him.'

Instead of shifting back, as he'd expected, she leaned further into the car. Tom tightened his lips to stop himself from yelling at her. She was doing her job, and doing it well, but that didn't stop him wanting to pull her out of the car, get her to safety.

'Andy, can you move your legs?' Not by the tiniest quiver did her voice betray any concern.

'No.' The word was more of a moan. 'It hurts.'

By the time Tom strode to the other side of the car and wrenched open the passenger door, Kayla had her arm pushed down into the well beneath the dashboard.

'Can you feel that, Andy?'

'Y-yes.'

'Where am I touching you?'

'Leg. Shin.'

'That's great.' She withdrew her arm and shone her pencil torch into the cramped space.

Newspaper crinkled under Tom's knee as he knelt on the seat and leaned across to reach under the driver's seat.

'Be careful,' Kayla said sharply. A heady mixture of whisky fumes and her light, spicy perfume assaulted his nostrils. 'There's glass from a broken bottle.'

'Thanks.' Tom winced at the gravelly catch in his voice.

'Andy's legs are caught under the dash. Apart from his ankle pain, there's no other obvious injury but visibility isn't great. I can't tell if he's trapped or just wedged forward with the seat.' She looked up, her wide eyes on a level with his for a breathless second. 'We can't shift him until we can straighten his legs and see. Before we try to move him out of the car, I'd like to try and shift the seat back so I can assess any lower limb damage properly.'

'Shift the seat. Right.' Tom drew in a lungful of air when her eyes swivelled back to Andy.

'Can you wriggle your toes for me, Andy?' she said, calmly carrying on with her examination.

'Y-yeah.'

'Are you allergic to any medications?'

'No.'

'Do you take medication for anything? Diabetes? Heart condition?'

'N-no. Need something for the p-pain.'

'Okay. You're doing great, Andy. I'll get you something for your pain now.' She turned away for a moment then was back with a vial and syringe in her hands. With the slender capping sheath clamped between her teeth, she filled the syringe. Tom blinked. He'd seen the paramedics use the same technique countless times. But somehow Kayla's even, white teeth performing the familiar action was unbelievably sexy.

As she plunged the needle into Andy's leg, Tom shook himself mentally and reached across to grope for the lever under the driver's seat. 'I'm going to move the seat back as far as I can, Kayla.'

'Sure.'

He jiggled the lever. Nothing. Applied more pressure. Still nothing. The angle was awkward. He moved further forward, closer to Kayla. Closer to her evocative female scent. *Concentrate.* He braced his knee uncomfortably on the handbrake and yanked directly upward.

The chair slid back with a jerk. Andy moaned.

'Sorry, mate,' said Tom.

Kayla was there in an instant. 'Where is your pain, Andy?'

'Ankle. Still.'

Tom edged back outside. The deadly petrol fumes were

stronger. They had to hurry. He clambered in behind the driver's seat. 'I'm going to lower the seat so we can take him out through the back.'

He wound the reclining mechanism with quick flicks of his wrist. 'Nearly ready to move him?'

She nodded, her mind obviously on the job as her voice sounded distracted when she spoke to him. 'Just let me make sure both his legs are free.'

There was a small popping noise.

'Hell.' Tom was moving as a terrifying whoosh followed. 'Kayla! Get out! Now!'

He scooped up the fire extinguisher, pulling the pin as he ran to the flames that leapt out of the gap between the crumpled bonnet and the front fender.

Aiming the nozzle, he pulled the trigger. The fire retreated, beaten into temporary submission. Moving forward, with a sweeping motion, Tom covered as much of the engine as he could with the foam. As soon as the cylinder started to splutter, he threw it aside and spun back towards the cabin of the car.

Kayla was still there. She hadn't done as he'd asked. Far from it, she'd taken his place in the rear of the car and had finished lowering the driver's seat. She was struggling to move Andy.

'I don't know how long that will hold.' He grabbed her by the upper arm, tugged her aside then slid in to take her place. 'We have to do this now.'

'We really need more hands,' she said, for the first time sounding anxious.

'We haven't got them. Come on, Kayla. Don't fold on me now.' He threaded his hands under Andy's armpits and locked his fingers across the man's chest. 'I'm going to pull him out. You try to ease his legs as they come free.'

'Got it.'

'Let's do it.' He grinned at her and could swear the corners of her mouth moved in a quick response.

'Andy? This is going to be uncomfortable but we need to pull you out of the car now.' It was the best he could do to prepare the victim for what had to be done.

'P-please. Get me out. D-don't leave me here.'

'We won't, mate.'

Tom moved back, taking the man's weight, feeling the resistance and straining past it. Andy groaned. Tom had to steel himself against the agony in the sound. If he left Andy here, there was every chance the man could die in the car.

Kayla had grabbed the thick newspaper from the passenger seat and she used it to support Andy's lower leg as his limb came free. In a move like a circus contortionist, she climbed onto the driver's seat, then over and through the back door, the whole time cradling Andy's injured ankle in the makeshift splint.

Between them, they carried Andy across the road.

'Behind my vehicle, Kayla. It'll give us some protection if the car goes up.'

They lowered a shivering Andy to the ground. Tom opened the back door of his vehicle and took out a blanket. 'Here.'

'Thanks,' Kayla said as she tucked it around Andy's body. 'I need my bag.'

'I'll get it.'

Tom paused for a second as she bent over her patient, getting straight back into the job, her fingers on Andy's wrist. 'How are you feeling, Andy?'

She was a real trooper, brave and resourceful. Damn, that was attractive. His heart swelled. He was…proud of her.

She looked around, one eyebrow shooting up as though she was surprised to see him. 'My bag, Sergeant?'

'Coming right up.' He smiled wryly, feeling chastened and deservedly so. She distracted the hell out of him.

He loped back to the wreck and grabbed her medical kit.

The still-strong smell of petrol, coupled with the sizzle of foam on hot metal, was ominous. His prevention measures were still holding but he didn't know for how long. He turned and ran back.

'Here.'

'Thanks.' She reached for the bag as soon as he put it beside her.

'I'll call it in,' Tom said, reaching into the cabin of his four-wheel drive and grabbing the radio handpiece.

'It's Senior Sergeant Tom Jamieson, Dustin Police.' He turned to watch Kayla bandaging a more stable splint on Andy's leg. Her long, clever fingers were quick and efficient. She moved with such grace and competence as she went about her business that Tom was hard pressed to take his eyes off her.

He swallowed and dragged his mind back to his report. 'I need fire and ambulance to a single-vehicle accident on the Valley Highway, west of Dustin. About ten kilometres out of town, nearest intersecting road Reece Lane.

'We've got one injured male, approximately forty-five, possible broken ankle. Doctor on scene providing first aid now.'

He looked over the bull bar of his vehicle towards the wreck. 'The situation is extremely hazardous. One full foam extinguisher has already been discharged to control fire in the motor vehicle's engine. It could reignite at any time.'

'Sergeant?' Kayla barked behind him. Tom turned to see her stripping the blanket off Andy. Her patient was clutching at his chest, his face twisted into a ghastly grimace. Then he collapsed, his arms slumping to his sides.

Kayla leaned over the now inert body, her fingers groping for a neck pulse.

'He's arresting. I need your assistance, stat. Get the resus mask out of my bag.' Kayla's hands were already in the middle of Andy's chest, the heels pumping down hard. 'Hurry.'

Tom let go of the handpiece and dropped to his knees beside the medical bag.

'That's it,' Kayla said as he lifted out a clear plastic mask with a pale green bag attached. 'Over his mouth and nose. Tilt his head back slightly. A solid puff now. And another.'

Tom did as he was directed.

'Good. Two breaths each thirty compressions. I'll count.' She kept up the rhythmic pressing.

It was the first time Tom had seen chest compressions performed on a live patient and it was a much more brutal process than he'd realised.

'Get ready.' Kayla's voice snapped his attention back. 'Twenty-eight, twenty-nine, Thirty. Again now.'

The radio dangling at the side of the car crackled. 'Sergeant Jamieson? Are you still receiving, over?' Tom ignored the tinny voice as he held the mask and squeezed the bag, forcing the air out into Andy.

Turning, he grabbed the radio, clicked the button and barked, 'Here, Dispatch. The accident vic is having a heart attack.'

Press. Press. 'Twenty-seven, Twenty-eight.'

Tom dropped the handpiece and got ready.

'Twenty-nine. Thirty, now.'

As soon as he'd done his bit, he snatched up the handpiece again. 'We're doing CPR.'

'Roger, Sergeant. Ambulance and fire are on their way. I'll update them. Over.'

'Twenty-nine. Thirty, now.'

The seconds crawled by, turning into minutes as they moved in a bizarre choreography. He rapped out short staccato snips of information on the radio then returned to pump air into Andy's lungs. Kayla placed her fingers on Andy's neck then returned to her compressions.

She worked tirelessly, her slender arms taut, hands linked. With each compression, her hair bobbed on her shoulders, swinging with her exertion. Light caught on the wheat-coloured strands. Tom was intensely aware of her every move. She was a competent, assured expert. If Andy died it wouldn't be because of anything that Kayla failed to do for him.

Three minutes.

Five minutes.

Kayla laid her fingers against Andy's neck, felt the reassuring bump in the carotid artery. 'Okay, we have a pulse.'

Out of the corner of her eye, she saw the policeman sink back on his heels and lift the handset. 'Dispatch, the victim has a pulse.'

Kayla felt an odd shiver as she let the deep, calm voice wash over her. She shook her head. She was tired, her muscles trembling with fatigue in the aftermath of the adrenalin-charged situation. The tremors were nothing to do with a deep, dark, baritone voice.

The unit crackled. 'Thank you, Sergeant. They should be with you shortly. Standing by.'

She looked at the profile of the man who'd been helping her. Dustin's police sergeant. The strong jaw with a shadow of whiskers on his cheeks. He looked stern and forbidding with the black T-shirt clinging to his chest and sculpted biceps. Much as she loathed large, muscle-bound men, she had to be thankful he'd been here tonight. She'd never have got Andy out of the car on her own.

She swallowed and turned her attention back to her patient. She tucked Andy's arm along his body and reached across for his other one. 'We should turn Andy into the recovery position.'

There was a faint wail of sirens in the distance, creeping closer.

'Going to be sick,' Andy slurred.

'We need to roll him,' she said urgently. 'I'll support his neck, you roll him towards me. My command, on three. Got

it? Okay. One, two, three.' Kayla fired out the order as she
held Andy's head.

And then the sour smell of vomit as Andy disgorged his
stomach contents over the knee of her trousers. She swallowed
the gag reflex that threatened. 'Okay, let's settle him so I can
clean him up. Gently, gently.'

'Wha's happen...?' Andy struggled to move as she slipped
a folded towel under his head.

'Just stay still for me, Andy.' She kept her hand firmly on
his shoulder, held him steady as she spoke. 'You've had an
accident. We're getting help for you.'

The sirens were closer.

'The cavalry's on its way,' Tom murmured, his rich, gravelly voice sliding over her.

'Amen to that.'

She looked up to find shadowed eyes on her.

And then he smiled. A simple curve of his mouth and his
face was transformed. Sergeant Jamieson was a very, very
attractive man. Kayla's heart squeezed hard.

Too much man for her to handle, whispered a confidence-
sapping inner voice. Too much, too big. Too hard.

Andy moved under her hand. With relief, she wrenched her
gaze away from the disturbing man opposite her patient.

CHAPTER TWO

THE smell of smoke drifted on the still air. Tom leaned sideways to look around the end of his car. Flames licked around the front tyre of the wreck.

As he got to his feet, the Dustin fire truck slid between him and his view of the fledgling fire. Thank God. He felt the tension ease across his shoulders.

A paramedic ran up to join Kayla as the ambulance backed slowly towards them. It stopped a couple of metres away and the second medic came around to open the back doors. Tom stood and moved back to give them more room. He watched a moment as Kayla meshed smoothly with the men, working to stabilise their patient.

Feeling superfluous, he crossed to the back of his four-wheel drive to take out the camera, tape measure and notepad. With his gear in hand, he walked around to the other side of the fire truck. The team had the wreck and surrounding area well doused with foam.

'Tom.' Dustin's fire captain, Jack Campbell, nodded to him then turned back to look at the crumpled car. 'How's your vic?'

'Looks like he'll make it, thanks to Kayla.'

'Lucky she was on hand.'

'Yeah.' Tom stared at the wreck, remembering the frenetic

light and sound show in the seconds before the crash. 'Even luckier she wasn't involved in the accident.'

'What happened?' Jack's voice was sharp with concern.

'I need to have a good look at the tyre marks and take her statement.' Tom lifted his shoulder. 'But I'd say she did some pretty fancy driving to avoid a collision. It'll have to be confirmed but indications are that the driver is alcohol-impaired.'

Jack grunted his disgust.

'Yeah.' Tom sighed heavily. 'I'm going to take some photos, make a few measurements for my report. I won't get in your way.'

'Sure. I called Dennis. He's on his way with the tow truck.' Hands on hips, Jack pointed his chin at the wreck. 'We're under control here but we'll hang around to make sure there are no flare-ups when the car's pulled off the tree trunk.'

'Thanks.'

Tom moved away and began snapping photographs from different angles. Inside the car, he took several pieces of the broken whisky bottle, making sure he got a clear shot of the label.

From a vantage point to one side, he made a quick sketch of the scene, placing the cars. On a walk along the road with his torch, he identified the skid marks—Andy's coming onto the main road from the lane; Kayla's where she'd braked and swerved to avoid him.

He could see quite clearly how the incident had unfolded. The tyre tracks told the story. Thick black rubber lines on the sealed road segued into gouges in the gravel verge before spiralling back onto the tarmac again. Just traversing the two vastly different road surfaces in a *straight* line was enough to bring many motorists to disaster. It was nothing short of a miracle that her little car hadn't rolled with the massive forces it had been under.

By concentrating on his job, he could prevent himself from thinking about how close Kayla had been to injury or death.

He laid out the measuring tape then jotted in distances on his sketch. With everything he needed for his report, he glanced over the road as he wound the tape up.

The paramedics were wheeling Andy to the back of the ambulance. Kayla was turned away from him, bent double as she wiped a towel down one leg.

Tom inhaled deeply then let the air out through his pursed lips in a silent whistle. The unimpeded view of her shapely bottom in the soft draping material of her trousers was very fine. Very fine indeed.

He wrenched his gaze away, looked down at the equipment in his hands. He wanted to talk to her...sensibly. Which was going to be a tough assignment if he couldn't rein in his physical response.

He gathered his thoughts. They'd made a connection here tonight and he wanted to build on that, not give her any chance, any excuse, to draw back. He'd seen a different side to her as she'd dealt with Andy. Brave, resourceful, competent—and he liked it. A lot.

Holding fast to those thoughts, he refused to succumb to further masculine appreciation of the view as he crossed the road.

'Kayla.'

She straightened abruptly—staggered slightly.

'Oh...no.' Her words were a small, useless protest as she slowly pitched forward.

Tom took the last two steps to her side, catching her to his chest. 'Steady, I've got you.'

'Sorry, sorry,' she mumbled. 'D-don't know what happened... Must have...stood too quickly.'

She didn't resist as he stepped her over to a small tree stump and lowered her to sit. He bent over her and pushed her head between her knees, acutely conscious of the soft, warm skin of her neck beneath his fingers. After a minute, she struggled against his pressure.

'I'm all right. Thank you, Sergeant.' Her voice sounded strangled.

'Tom.'

'Anything. Whatever.' He felt her convulsive shudder as she turned her head towards him, her eyes closed. 'Please. All I can smell is the vomit on my knee.'

'Oh. Sorry, I forgot.' He released her, his grip supporting her as she sat up straight. Silky strands of hair teased the back of his hand. She took a quick breath and swallowed audibly. 'Just sit a minute.'

He kept a hand on her nape as he called to the paramedic who had just backed out of the back of the ambulance and was closing the doors. 'Gaz? Can you take Kayla back with you for a once-over?'

'Sure, no problem.'

Beneath his palm, he could feel the delicate shifting of muscle as Kayla shook her head.

'That's not necessary, Sergeant. I—'

He looked back at her. 'I think it is, Kayla. You were a hair's breadth from being involved in a nasty accident tonight. And the name is Tom.' If she called him Sergeant one more time tonight, he'd plant a kiss right on that luscious mouth and completely ruin her opinion of him.

'But I need my car.' She looked mutinous, her silver eyes glowing with irritation.

'And I'll see that you get it,' he said as he stood. 'For now, I'm impounding it.'

Her mouth opened.

He bent, slipping one arm around her shoulders, the other under her knees and scooped her up. Her mouth snapped shut on a small squeak as she grabbed at his shoulder to steady herself. He smiled grimly. His hands were on Kayla and he couldn't do a thing about it. Torture. He looked down on the curve of lashes on her cheek, the gentle swell of her breasts...

the fist in her lap. He'd take no bets on where she'd like to plant it.

He was a masochist.

'Open your front passenger door for me, Gaz.'

'Sure thing, Tom.' Gary grinned as he opened the door wide.

Tom shovelled his armful of warm woman onto the seat, wondering if his reluctance to let her go was obvious to anyone other than him.

God, he had to get out of here before he made an idiot of himself. He stepped back quickly and cleared the congestion from his throat.

'Buckle up, Doc,' he said as he shut the door.

Kayla's narrow-eyed glare should have sizzled his skin. At least her anger had brought some colour to her pallid cheeks. A little hectic but colour just the same.

Tom pivoted and strode over to where Jack Campbell was rolling up the hose. The bonnet of the car had been wrenched open and the engine was now well doused with fire-retardant foam.

'Kayla okay?' asked Jack.

'She says so.' Tom avoided his friend's shrewd eyes. 'I've sent her back with the ambos for a check over.'

'And she was okay with that?'

'Sure. Why wouldn't she be?' Tom set his jaw and ignored the laughter he could see in Jack's face. 'I'll get one of your guys to drive her car back to the hospital when we go, if that's okay?'

'Sure. Might as well be me. I want to roust Liz out. She should have been home a couple of hours ago.'

'Good luck with that.'

'Yeah.' Jack chuckled.

Kayla sucked another deep breath into her oxygen-deprived lungs. Her diaphragm had frozen from the moment the sergeant had lifted her. Making a conscious effort to ease her tension, she uncurled the fists in her lap. Her short practical nails had dug into the soft tissue, leaving small red dints in her palm.

Even with his disturbing presence gone, she could still feel his touch. Hard enough when it had just been his hand on her nape, strong fingers clasped gently on her neck, the rasp of his calloused skin while he'd been holding her head down. Being clasped to his chest, surrounded by his warmth and strength…the awareness of her female softness against the hardness of his muscular frame had overwhelmed her.

The honest, earthy scent of him, a smell that owed more to a hard day's work than scientists testing essences in a laboratory, seemed to call to her in a way that was disturbing, primitive. She'd always liked men to be well groomed, wearing a subtle, musky aftershave. Yet no one she'd dated had ever affected her as profoundly as this man in his snug jeans and a simple black T-shirt.

Thank goodness he didn't realise he was responsible for her light-headed state. Or at least partially responsible. If she'd eaten a proper meal before leaving Melbourne, if she hadn't straightened from her bent position so quickly. If he hadn't crept up on her, spoken her name so unexpectedly. Panic had made her head jerk upright, had flooded her system with an explosion of contrary stimuli. Instead of doing anything sensible, she'd nearly pitched face down at his feet. Would have if he hadn't caught her.

Which brought her full circle back to being held in his arms. She shivered.

What was it about his brand of masculinity that left her dizzy with all sorts of chaotic feelings? Whatever it was, she didn't like the feeling of vulnerability. There were so many strikes against him. A career police officer, strong and hard. Controlled and used to controlling. She had to find a way to cram the sergeant back into the mental box she'd managed to keep him in for the two months she'd been living in Dustin.

He'd said she should call him Tom. She didn't even want to *think* about him that personally…intimately. Ridiculous though it was, if she thought of him as *Tom*, he'd become too real, a man she'd have to deal with. As Sergeant Jamieson, he was a police officer, someone she could keep at a distance. She was only here for another four months. Surely she could lock her unruly reactions down long enough to get through that.

She rolled her head to look at him where he stood with Jack Campbell. Both were long, lean, athletic men. Two of a kind. Yet she'd never felt threatened by Jack. He was a honey. She knew he and Liz had had their problems but they'd come through them and now their marriage was stronger than ever. They were a family, one adorable daughter and another baby on the way.

Sergeant Jamieson was a different proposition altogether. He had hot eyes. At the few social occasions she'd attended, she'd felt him watching her. He'd never put a foot wrong, but in her mind he was disturbing. Radiating a hunger that she didn't want to think about. For things that weren't his, things he had no right to. She shivered again. He made her feel utterly conscious of her vulnerability as a woman.

She mentally shook herself. It didn't matter what he wanted. What *she* wanted was what counted. And she didn't want any man in her life at the moment.

And definitely not someone like Sergeant Tom Jamieson.

CHAPTER THREE

Tom fell into step with Jack as they walked towards the bright lights at the hospital entrance.

'Here are Kayla's keys.' Jack held out his hand.

'Thanks,' Tom said, spotting his quarry as soon as he stepped through the sliding door into the emergency department.

Tall and straight in the shapeless green theatre pants and top, Kayla still looked entirely too appealing. Her pale face turned towards them. When she realised it was him, an interesting shade of pink bloomed along her cheek bones and her eyes darkened to stormcloud grey. He might have flattered himself that his appearance had that effect—except for the ferocious frown that pleated her forehead a split second later.

'Uh-oh, looks like you're in the dogbox, mate,' murmured Jack beside him as they walked towards her.

'Hey, Kayla.' Jack stooped to kiss her cheek.

'Hello, Jack.'

'Is Liz around?'

'She's in the tearoom with her feet up. I think she'll be glad to go home.'

'That's what I'm here for. Catch you two kids later.' Jack grinned at the two of them and winked.

Tom watched the expressions flit over her face as her eyes

followed Jack. Then suddenly she turned to face him, her silvery eyes impaling him, her mouth firm.

'My keys, please, Sergeant?'

He juggled them in his hands, tossing them from one to the other. 'Have you been cleared by your doctor...*Doctor*?'

'Yes, of course.'

He tilted his head and considered her. 'So, your near collapse was because...?'

Her lips thinned and for a moment he thought she'd refuse to answer. He almost relished the opportunity to lock horns with her.

'Low blood sugar. Tiredness. Getting up too quickly. I prescribed myself a cup of tea and grilled cheese on toast while I waited for you to return my keys.' She held out her hand. 'And now I'd like to go home to bed.'

Tom's fingers clutched the keys as he bit back a tempting retort. She did *not* mean anything by her comment. It was *not* an opening or an offer. If he was a gentleman, he would definitely let that slide through to the keeper.

He cleared his throat and dangled the keys. 'In that case...'

As she reached out, he caught her hand, gently turning it over and depositing the keys on her palm with studied care. He curled her fingers over them one at a time as he held her eyes with his.

'Thank you.' She tugged lightly and when he didn't release her, she narrowed her eyes at him. 'Was there something else...Sergeant?'

'Yes, there is. Kayla.' He let his tongue linger over the syllables of her name. 'You get a good night's sleep.'

He felt her hand twitch in his, saw a flare of awareness in her eyes. And something else. A starkness, a vulnerability. Surely she wasn't afraid of him. He released his grip and her hand dropped to her side.

'Thank you, Sergeant.'

She turned away, walking quickly, her movements oddly jerky as though she was having trouble co-ordinating her limbs. As though she couldn't get away from him fast enough.

He wasn't used to having that sort of effect on women. He knew, without conceit, that he was reasonably good looking. Kayla Morgan was indifferent, immune. No, more than that—she seemed to find him downright distasteful. Damn it, she didn't know him well enough to feel that way about him. It rankled, made him want to get in her way, be hard to ignore.

Hands on hips, he watched until she was several metres away then he called softly, 'Kayla?'

The stiff stride halted. 'Yes?'

He waited, the silence stretched. She pivoted to look at him with obvious reluctance. 'What did you want?'

There it was again, that hint of defencelessness, of desperately masked fear. It reached out and touched him. Made him want to gather her close, shield her from whatever was troubling her. Which was difficult because he seemed to be the main cause of her stress right now. How could he protect her from himself?

'Come and see me at the station this week. I need you to make a statement about the accident.'

'Oh. Yes.' She swallowed, relief patent on her face. 'All right.'

'Goodnight.' He jammed his hands into the front pockets of his jeans.

''Night.' And she was moving away from him again. A couple of steps later she stopped. He could almost see an internal battle being waged as she looked over her shoulder then turned to face him. 'I should thank you for your assistance tonight.'

'Should you?'

'Yes, I should,' she said firmly, squaring her shoulders. Her bearing reminded him of his nephew's attitude when he'd had to apologise for a serious transgression. Courage, trepi-dation and determination not to flinch from an unpleasant task. No prizes for guessing what, or who, was the distasteful thing in this case. 'You were great at the accident. Thank you, Sergeant.'

'Happy to help...Doctor.'

With a quick nod, she spun around and moved away, with-out hesitating this time.

Why was he doing this to himself? Kayla was giving him red lights all the way. Yet he felt compelled to keep pushing, to try to get close.

She was confident and competent when doing her job, but so vulnerable and prickly with him when dealing with him on a personal level.

He watched until she moved out of sight without looking back then he huffed out a breath. He'd thought she might look back at him, give him some indication that she knew he was still standing there. A vain hope.

He hunched his shoulders. Perhaps he should back off, let it go. Kayla was Liz's friend. Liz would skewer him if he upset her. The whole thing was complicated.

'Earth to Tom?'

He turned to find Liz watching him, curiosity and concern in her eyes. He wondered how long she'd been standing there, what she'd read on his face. She glanced along the corridor to where Kayla had disappeared.

'Jack was looking for you,' he said quickly into the brief silence.

'He found me. Tony just collared him about something so I came on ahead.' She paused. 'We stabilised your accident victim and sent him off to Melbourne. I organised that blood test for his alcohol level, too.'

'Good, thanks.'

'Tom...about Kayla...'

'What about her?' He tried to sound casual but knew he hadn't succeeded by Liz's troubled expression.

'Tom, I love you very dearly and I'm telling you as a friend... Kayla's not up to your weight.'

'I don't know what you mean.'

'Don't you?' she said dryly. 'I've seen the way you look at her. And not just today.'

'Well, she's not looking back so you can put your mind at ease.'

'Perhaps.' Liz looked along the corridor again. 'Kayla's my friend, Tom.'

'I know. I'm just having a hard time picturing the two of you as pals. You seem like an unlikely pair.'

'She came to my rescue when a charming date spiked my drink. I was in first year at uni and pretty green. Kayla stood up to him and took me to hospital. She looked after me, Tom, even though we didn't know each other.' Liz's eyes examined his face as she spoke. 'She didn't have to get involved and yet she chose to. She was a better friend to me that night than all my so-called close friends.'

He rubbed his jaw. This picture of the valiant, loyal, caring Kayla was incredibly attractive. All the qualities a man could ask for in a potential life partner.

'Why is she here in Dustin?'

'You know why she's here.' Liz patted her protruding stomach and looked smug. 'She's working while I'm on maternity leave.'

'But you're not on leave yet.'

'True.' She tilted her head and looked up at him for a long moment. Her eyebrows rose. 'Why don't you ask her?'

He grimaced. 'I would if she wasn't so damned prickly. She *Sergeants* me to death and treats me like I've got her under bright lights for interrogation.'

'You can be intimidating.'

'Nah.' He smiled at her. 'I'm a SNAG.'

She gave him a droll look. 'I've yet to meet anyone less like a sensitive new-age guy than you. Except maybe Jack.'

Tom laughed. 'Then I'm in good company.' He waited a beat then said, 'So how about it? What's her story?'

Liz looked at him thoughtfully. 'You know I won't tell you that. But I will tell you that it suited both of us for her to come to Dustin early.' She smoothed her hand over her stomach, a small smile on her mouth. 'And when my time comes, I know I'm in safe hands with Kayla.'

He grinned as he saw Liz's husband approaching. 'Not getting Jack to play midwife for this one?'

'He's on standby. But even he admits he'll be happy to take a back seat for the arrival of future Campbells.' She grinned up at her husband as he slipped his arm around her waist. 'Won't you, darling?'

'Believe it. You, my sweet, are confined to town for the rest of your pregnancy. A maximum of two kilometres from the hospital at all times.'

'Uh-uh. There's the camp draft next weekend. You promised.'

'Only because Kayla's going. And only because it's within my fail-safe ten-kilometre radius from the hospital.'

The look that passed between his friends was one of such pure delight that Tom's heart squeezed. He wanted a woman to look at him like that, as though he was the most important man in her world.

And not just any woman.

He wanted it to be Kayla.

Kayla tugged the front of her shirt, suddenly wishing she'd worn something more substantial than her favourite red shirt. She'd never realised how low the front was, not that it showed cleavage but the respectable square neckline showed an alarming amount of her décolletage. All that bare skin suddenly seemed outrageously provocative. The short, cap sleeves left her arms bare and somehow vulnerable.

And it was red. Sure, it suited her. She'd worn it because red was the colour of confidence and she needed all of that commodity she could muster for this interview. But the colour also screamed, *Look over here, look at me* in a way that she'd never appreciated before.

If it weren't for the fact that she was actually standing on the veranda of the police station, she'd have fled home to change her blouse for something black that covered her from hyoid bone to scaphoid. She looked around surreptitiously and, sure enough, there was a security camera at the corner of the roof line. Great, now she probably looked like she was about to commit a felony.

She'd put off this moment as long as she could. The simple task of making the statement had grown into a task of monumental proportions. All she was doing was giving her version of events, for heaven's sake. A formality. It wasn't as if the accident was her fault. She'd been sober, driving carefully, and her quick evasive actions had prevented an even more serious situation.

As for Sergeant Jamieson…he was just a man. Doing a job. He wouldn't bite. He probably wouldn't even be the person she'd have to deal with so she was getting herself into a lather for nothing. She needed to get a grip, tell the person taking her statement what had happened, answer a few questions. Simple.

She took a deep breath, straightened her shoulders then pushed open the door of the police station.

'Hey, Kayla.'

'Penny. Hi.' Kayla grinned at the neatly uniformed woman on duty behind the counter. The tension in her stomach began to smooth out. She could talk to Penny, give her statement, get on the road to Melbourne. She didn't need to see the sergeant. Reprieve!

'I hear you've got a new fan.' Penny smiled.

'Fan?'

'My niece. Suzy MacIntyre. You saw her the other day.'

'Oh, of course. She's a delight.'

'Isn't she? She was telling me all about her visit to see you. And how brave she was about her injection and the jelly-bean she chose and the cute little animal stamp you gave her. You know she wouldn't let poor Sarah wash it off for ages. They had to bathe her and wash around it.'

'Oh, dear.'

'Now she wants to come back to see you. She said she'd even have another injection if she had to.'

Kayla chuckled.

'Anyway, you probably haven't come by to listen to the ramblings of a proud aunty.' Penny clicked her fingers. 'Oh, I bet you're here about Andy's accident last week.'

'I'm always happy to listen to proud aunty tales. But, yes, I've come to make a statement.'

'Tom won't be long. He's just on a phone call at the moment. Want a coffee?'

'No, thanks. Do you think…well, could I give you the statement?'

Penny looked doubtful. 'Tom was very specific about wanting to see you himself. Which is a bit unusual really for something so routine.'

'It'd be a shame to disturb him.'

'Uncommonly thoughtful of you, Kayla.'

The deep voice made her jump. Spinning to her left, she met the sergeant's knowing dark gaze. Heat swept her from head to toe and she felt as though she'd been caught planning something criminal.

He smiled at her. 'I'm free now. All yours, in fact.'

The skin over her cheek bones was scorching as every particle of heat concentrated in her face. If only it was enough to combust her on the spot.

The dark, narrow-eyed stare raked over her already sensitised skin. 'You're looking better than when I last saw you.'

The personal comment allowed her to pull herself together. 'Really, Sergeant?'

'Tom. No need to stand on ceremony around here, is there, Penny?' He smiled warmly at his constable and Kayla's thought processes stuttered to a halt.

He looked back at her. 'Want to come this way?'

No. She swallowed and forced her jellied knees to move her forward. The tension in her gut returned with an iron fist, making her glad it had been hours since she'd eaten.

Her heart set up a tattoo of great thumping beats as she followed him along a short corridor. She worked to compose herself, using the techniques that had served her so well for years when dealing with the large threatening males in her life. The usual methods weren't working.

'Grab a chair.' He moved behind the desk to open a filing cabinet and take out a pad.

She perched on the edge of the seat and concentrated on the items on his desk. It was all very tidy. Orderly piles of paper, a container of pens.

Long fingers appeared in her line of vision, selected one of the pens and clicked it ready for use.

'Tell me in your own words what happened last Sunday night, Kayla. You were returning from Melbourne?' His smooth, velvety voice invited her to respond.

'Y-yes.' She marshalled her thoughts and began to describe the accident.

He made notes as she spoke.

'So you didn't see the lights of the car coming down the side road towards you?' His dark eyes lifted to her face.

The question brought her up short.

'No. I was…um…distracted.' On that fateful night, she'd spotted him. In her mind's eye, she could remember the tall, still figure beside the police vehicle. She'd wondered what he was doing out there in the middle of the night. Heat crept up her neck and it was all she could do not to put her hand to her throat to try to hide the self-betrayal. 'I had glanced in the side mirror. The—the right-hand one on the...' She stopped. 'Right side.'

She was giving too much information, too much detail. Making herself sound like an idiot. Worse, she was drawing his attention and surely making him wonder what she was hiding.

Just as well she'd never contemplated a life of crime. Giving one tiny statement under Sergeant Jamieson's piercing eyes was turning her into a gibbering wreck.

'And then what happened?'

'I—I looked back and the other car was suddenly there, at my left-hand passenger door. I braked hard and swerved to the right side of the road. My car spun when I hit the gravel.'

He led her through several more questions, then she watched as he finished making his notes.

'Okay, that seems straightforward. I'll just get you to read through this and sign if you're happy with what it says.'

'Okay.' She took the pages. The short, terse sentences in his powerful, energetic script seemed to leap off the paper at her. She blinked and forced herself to concentrate. 'I just sign at the bottom?'

'Yes. You can use my pen.'

The pen was still warm from his fingers. She leaned the paper on the edge of the desk to scrawl her signature then handed the papers back to him.

'So that's it?'

'Pretty much.' He looked at her. 'How about a coffee?'

'Coffee?'

'Yes. I wouldn't expect you to drink the station coffee if that's what you're worried about.' He smiled but his eyes were dark, unreadable.

'Oh, I'm sure it couldn't be as bad as hospital coffee.' She stopped, bit her lip. He'd think she wanted to stay for coffee in a minute. 'Thank you, but, no. I need to get on the road. I've got a long drive.'

'Going to Melbourne for the weekend?'

'Yes.' She gathered up her belongings and decided she'd get her car keys out when she got to her car.

His face was perfectly calm but there was an acuteness about the way he looked at her that made her wonder what he was thinking. Perhaps all policemen cultivated that impression of predatory patience. Waiting to see what might be revealed if they waited long enough. 'Visiting family?'

'Yes. No. Sort of.' Her fingers tightened on her bag.

He raised his eyebrows.

She opened her mouth then shut it. He couldn't possibly be interested in knowing this was her best friend's last weekend in Melbourne before she returned to the far-flung reaches of North West Australia.

His curiosity was a policeman's ingrained habit and she was like Pavlov's dog. A steady stare from an imposing male wearing dark blue epaulettes and it seemed she was still ready to rush into explanations. Her father had trained her well.

Growing up, she'd tried to tell herself it was a sign of his affection that had made him grill her and her sister. But she'd slowly realised it was an uncanny ability to sniff out the tiniest hint of trouble or rebellion.

A fantastic ability in a policeman.

Utterly crushing in a distant, regimented father.

In the end, she'd realised he'd been determined to crush any tendency his daughters might have harboured towards behaving like normal teenagers. Christopher Morgan had been a man with places to go, in line for promotions. No time for messy family dramas and misbehaviour. No taint of gossip would touch him through his family.

She suddenly realised she'd been sitting in the sergeant's

office for far too long, staring back at him. She shot out of the chair. 'Well, I won't let you keep me.'

'Won't you?' He stood more slowly, his eyes hooded, a faint smile on his mouth.

She felt the heat rush into her cheeks when she realised what she'd said. 'I mean, I won't keep you.'

He inclined his head. 'I'll walk you out.'

'There's no need. I can find my own way. Thank you, Sergeant.'

'Tom.' His fingers fastened around her arm.

She looked at him blankly, her mind consumed by his touch on the tender skin of her inner elbow.

'My name is Tom.'

'Oh. Yes. Of course.' She looked at him helplessly.

'Say it, Kayla.'

She swallowed. The way he said her name sent a shiver down her spine. Almost as though he was tasting the syllables, trying out the feel of it in his mouth. At the L-sound, she'd been able to see the tip of his tongue touch the edge of his top teeth.

'Say it,' he repeated when she remained silent.

'Tom.' Her throat had difficulty making the sound and it came out raw and husky. She'd worked so hard not to even think of him by his name, and now he'd made her say it. She felt something akin to despair. Now he was real, now he was a man, not a uniform.

He nodded. 'That wasn't so hard, was it?'

He opened his office door and ushered her across to the exit with that gentle but inexorable hold. Her feet moved her along beside him, across the veranda, down the steps to the side of her car. His fingers slid lightly across her elbow joint and finally released her.

He waited while she fumbled in her bag to find her keys to unlock the door. Then he leaned forward to open it for her. 'Drive carefully, Kayla. See you when you get back next week.'

Not if she saw him first. She slipped into the seat and managed to slide the key into the ignition.

'Bye, S—' She gulped the rest of the word when his eyes narrowed. 'Goodbye, Tom.'

He towered in the opening, one hand on the roof and the other on the door, as though he might say something more. But in the end all he said was, 'Bye, Kayla.'

He stepped back and shut the door gently.

As she stopped in the driveway to check the way was clear, she caught sight of him in her rear-vision mirror.

Thank goodness she drove an automatic car. It would just be the last straw to grind the gears or bunny-hop out onto the road under his watchful eye.

She didn't quite know what to make of Tom Jamieson.

But one thing was certain: he was a serious handicap to her enjoyment of Dustin.

CHAPTER FOUR

FROM his position in the corridor just outside the hospital cafeteria, Tom watched Kayla through the glass window and listened with half an ear to his sister's plans for the coming weekend. Kayla turned from the counter and threaded her way through the tables.

'Tom!'

'What?' He looked down at his sister's indignant features.

'You haven't heard a thing I've said, have you?'

He arched an eyebrow. 'Mum's still jet-lagged after travelling back from England on Tuesday and you're concerned about her overdoing it at the barbecue on Saturday night,' he said smugly and glanced back into the cafeteria as he spoke. Kayla had selected a seat by the window. 'You've arranged for Dad to get the meat and everyone else to bring salads and sweets.' He looked back at Charlotte, who gave him a narrow-eyed glare. 'Am I right?'

'Do you know how irritating it is when you can do that?'

'What? Prove I've been listening?'

'Mmm.' She craned her neck to look into the cafeteria. Tom had an overwhelming urge to block her line of sight to Kayla. 'What's so interesting anyway?'

He was saved from answering by the piercing beep of

Charlotte's pager. 'Damn. Got to run. See you on Saturday night, then.'

'Sure thing.'

Thankful for the narrow escape, he pushed open the door and headed towards Kayla. A moment later, her head came up, eyes darting around the room as though she'd sensed imminent danger. No mistaking the dismay on her face as her gaze settled on him. He suppressed a sigh. Nothing had changed— he was a sucker for punishment. Continuing towards her, he set his mouth in a grim smile. Her instinctive intention to bolt was plain. He wondered for a moment if he'd get some early cutting practice for the weekend camp draft—perversely, the thought made his smile broaden. Kayla sank back in her chair—he could practically see each muscle relax as she realised that flight was not an option.

She'd managed to avoid him for a couple of days, once in the supermarket and the other time at the library. And she hadn't returned the message he'd left her but that wasn't a surprise because he'd made it clear the message was private, not official. Perhaps he'd have to resort to something official to get a response.

A roadworthy check, a breathalyser set up outside the hospital just for a chance to talk to her. She was reducing him to a sad state.

But not today.

He tightened his grip on the bag he carried. Today, he had a cast-iron reason to see her. And plenty of time, too, since he knew she'd only just started her lunch break.

He stopped beside her table. 'Kayla.'

'Sergeant.'

He let that slide as he pulled out the chair on the diagonal from her and sat down, setting the bag on the floor. 'You're a hard woman to pin down.'

Her brows arched over darkly lashed grey eyes. 'I wasn't aware that I needed pinning.'

A glorious procession of X-rated images sprang unhelpfully into his mind and he could feel an unfamiliar warmth mushrooming in his face.

Hell, he was blushing.

He never blushed.

'You don't…er…need pinning.' He coughed to clear the huskiness from his vocal cords, all the while aware of her faintly perplexed expression. 'I've been trying to catch up with you.'

'I know. I got your message but it didn't seem urgent. Is there a problem with my statement about the accident?'

'Nope. No problem with that.'

'Good.' Her soft mouth pursed briefly and then she made a production of looking at her watch. 'I really should be getting…'

She trailed off as the cafeteria owner slipped a plate in front of her and then a cup of coffee. Tom stifled an urge to laugh at the comical look of guilt on her face.

'Hey, Tom,' said the woman with a smile. 'Can I get you anything?'

'A coffee would be great.'

'Black, no sugar, coming right up.'

He turned back to look at Kayla. 'Tsk, don't you know it's bad form to lie to a policeman?'

A strange spasm crossed her face. Pain? Then she lowered her eyes. 'Yeah, I do, as it happens.'

His interest sharpened but he left the questions unasked. Instead, he filed her response away with all the other things he wanted to know about her.

'I'll let you off this time.'

'Gee, thanks.' The sarcasm was unmistakeable as she lifted her eyes back to his.

He frowned and let his gaze roam over her face, watched with interest as she fidgeted and a tinge of pink crept into her cheeks. 'You know, if I was a suspicious man, I'd think you were avoiding me.'

She tilted her head to give him a considering look. The corner of her mouth crimped for a moment and then she said, 'You're a policeman. Suspicion is in your job description.'

'Okay. Good point,' he said, biting back the laugh that threatened. She had a quick wit and he was damned if bandying words with her wasn't wickedly good fun. Hoping to provoke another exchange, he reached over and snagged a chip off her plate. 'Eat up. Don't mind me, I've already eaten.'

'Not enough by the look of it,' she said as he blew on the chip.

'Always room for a chip or two.' He popped it in his mouth.

'In that case, do feel free to help yourself,' she said, her tone withering as she picked up her knife and fork.

He grinned and grabbed another. 'I hear you're going to the camp draft this weekend.'

She narrowed her eyes at him. 'Yes. I am.' She sounded reluctant to part with the details.

'With Liz and Jack?'

'Yes.'

'Looking forward to it?' he said, making a mental note to check with Jack to see if they intended to stay out at the grounds over the weekend. They did usually but with Liz being pregnant they might opt for the comfort of home and just drive out during the day.

'I'm sure it'll be interesting.' She pushed the grilled fish around on her plate then cut a small portion off the end. 'What was it you wanted to see me about?'

'I've got some gear for you from Penny. Boots and a hat.'

'Oh. I was going to pick it up from her tonight.'

He shrugged. 'I was coming this way so I offered to drop it off to you.' *Which was a long way from the truth. He'd prac-*

tically had to prise the bag out of his confused constable's fingers.

'Thanks.' She laid the knife and fork on her plate.

'My pleasure.' He looked at her substantially untouched food and frowned. 'Not hungry? You should eat more. There's nothing of you.'

More colour flooded into her cheeks and the grey eyes sparkled with irritation. 'Thank you for that professional assessment, Sergeant.'

'Tom. And it's not a complaint. What there is of you is a very nice package.' He knew he was out of line but something about seeing her mouth open in a perfect oval of outrage was irresistible. Baiting her like this was probably doing little to help his cause, but he couldn't seem to help himself. 'I wouldn't like to see you fade away while you're in Dustin.'

'Highly unlikely.' She gave him a fulminating glare from stormy grey eyes. 'Unless you're going to make a habit of dropping by to pilfer my lunch.'

'If that's an invitation, I accept.'

'It's not.'

'Shame. Well, much as I'd love to, I can't stay and chat. There's work to be done.' He pushed himself to his feet and lifted the bag onto the chair. 'Your accessories for the weekend. See you, Kayla.'

Not waiting for an answer, he walked towards the exit. A quick glance in the mirrored glass on the wall showed Kayla watching him leave. Perhaps he should check his shirt for scorch marks when he got back to the station.

He suppressed a grin. At least he could get under her skin. Not his first choice of reactions but it did mean she wasn't completely indifferent to him.

What had that been all about?

Kayla frowned. Since the accident, she seemed to have had

more to do with Tom Jamieson than for the entire time she'd been in Dustin prior to that.

She watched the door shut behind him then shifted her gaze to the bag on the chair beside her.

The knots in her stomach unravelled enough to allow a gurgle of hunger to escape.

She looked back at her plate and after a moment picked up the utensils. Stupid to let good food go to waste because the sergeant was so disturbing. Doggedly chewing a mouthful, she tried to banish him from her mind by thinking about the last patient she'd seen before lunch.

A sixty-year-old male, heavy smoker with a long-standing cough. He'd wanted a quick pass through the office and a script for antibiotics but she hadn't liked the wheezing sounds she'd heard in his lungs on auscultation. He hadn't liked her insistence on him having a chest X-ray.

Kayla sighed. She seemed to be bent on annoying the men who came into her orbit today. The expression in the sergeant's deep chocolate eyes had swung between frustration and puckish humour.

Except for those few moments when she could swear he looked embarrassed. He didn't strike her as the sort to be easily disconcerted. Her own system had been so jangled by his presence, she couldn't remember what they'd been talking about.

Her eyes slid back to the bag from Penny.

The weekend. Would Tom be at the camp draft? Her appetite abruptly evaporated and she had to force the food down her throat.

She reached for her coffee and took a swallow. She'd agreed to camp out at the grounds with Jack and Liz. Her first experience in a tent. She wasn't sure if she was dreading it or looking forward to it. Either way, having Sergeant Tom Jamieson around would only complicate things. He was a hard man to ignore when he got in her face.

She lifted her cup, then, as a sudden suspicion leapt into her mind, she froze with it halfway to her mouth. Surely he wasn't putting himself in her way deliberately.

No. Why would he?

She huffed out a sigh of impatience. In a minute, she'd be chewing her fingernails or twirling a hank of hair like a fourteen-year-old anguishing over the way a boy had looked at her.

So what if Tom Jamieson was there at the weekend. She'd just avoid him.

Easy. Now, if only she could get him out of her thoughts.

Picking up the fork again, she stabbed another piece of fish.

Who'd have thought she'd get such a kick out of the camp draft? Kayla grinned. The dust, the horses, the energetic noise of it, she loved it all. The people of Dustin were putting a touch of country into the city girl.

She looked down at herself and her good humour deepened. The dusty brown cargo pants, her most casual pair of trousers, and the long-sleeved cream shirt were her own. The scuffed elastic-sided boots on her feet and the felt hat perched on the seat beside her were on loan from Penny. Mandatory fashion wear for attending a camp draft event, she'd been told. When she'd dressed to drive out here this morning, she'd been self-conscious in her unfamiliar trimmings. Now they looked just right. She almost felt like the genuine article.

From her seat under the trees, she had a good view, although her position was on the opposite side of the arena to most of the action. People had stopped to chat through the morning and she'd gleaned helpful snippets of information.

She knew that right now the next competitor was in the small penned area known as the *camp* with a group of cows... *no, not plain old cows. For camp drafting, they were known as beasts.*

Tom Jamieson was judging this section of the competition. She'd lost count of the number of people who'd told her that. As if she needed to be told. Her eyes strayed again to the man on the large, sleepy-looking brown horse standing patiently beside the double gates of the camp.

Tom.

He sat in the saddle, loose and relaxed, with his attention on the action in the pen.

She dragged her gaze back to the gates, which would open any moment. The selected beast would bolt through with a hopeful rider in hot pursuit. Then with skill and perhaps a dollop of luck, the animal would be persuaded to gallop a figure-eight pattern around the saplings positioned in the arena.

The gates opened, but luck wasn't with the competitor. His beast evaded him, darting to its left and making a beeline along the fence.

After a few moments, the disqualification whistle sounded. Tom's horse perked up at some invisible command and cantered forward eagerly to herd the errant bovine towards the attendants. With a feeling of despair, Kayla watched the way Tom's body moved with the loping horse. That sinewy masculine strength moving in graceful partnership with the muscular animal beneath him appealed to a very basic corner of her psyche.

And it shouldn't.

She wanted to howl with frustration. She'd never had such a gut-wrenching response to a man before. The wicked brew of sensations left her reeling.

Why now?

Why him?

He was so unsuitable. Large and physical. Controlling. And a policeman. Three strikes.

She preferred her men to be medium-sized, medium-tempered and, after her recent experiences, anything *but* a career police officer.

The loudspeaker cracked to life. 'And that's the end of the novice section. We'll take a small break. Could competitors for the next category make sure they're mounted and ready? Thank you.'

Tom's head swivelled in her direction. His broad-brimmed hat sat low over his eyes, making it impossible to see his features, but that didn't stop a tiny shiver of awareness from lancing through her stomach. Stupid. He wasn't looking at her. Probably had no idea she was even there.

She picked up her hat, jammed it on her head and got to her feet.

She had to get away, give her system a chance to equilibrate. With Tom out of sight, she'd have more chance of banishing him from her mind. She turned away from the arena and strode across the packed-earth path beneath the trees, enjoying the crunch of dry leaves and twigs.

Jack had taken Liz back to their camp to put her feet up a while ago. Hopefully, he'd have some water heating for a billy tea. There! She'd leave Dustin with a new vocabulary as well as some wonderful memories.

She let her arms swing with each step as she sucked in another lungful of warm, morning air and savoured the clean sharp tang of eucalyptus oil.

Each exhalation seemed to clear away more of the fog of sadness and anxiety that had plagued her for the last six months. The betrayal of her fiancé and unceasing disapproval of her father seemed distant, unimportant things in this magical place beneath the gum trees. Even the worries about her sister eased.

In their stead, a marvellous sense of freedom. And a confirmation that she'd made the right decision by coming here to do the locum for Liz. The kilometres between the small country town and her family down in the city helped her to see how suffocating and unhealthy her relationships with them had become.

Ultimately, she would do what she could to heal the rifts with them. But for now she was content with her plans. After she'd finished in Dustin, she was moving on. Remote area medicine. On her weekends off, she'd already done some of the courses that would stand her in good stead, help her to qualify for a position. She was waiting on one final enrolment. With luck she'd pick up a place earlier if there was a cancellation.

No going back to the city. Dustin was the stepping stone to the rest of her life.

She was doing what was right for her, not what was expected.

The simplicity of being in this rural valley was like a balm to her spirit. The steep, treed hillsides of the natural basin, towering gum-leaf canopies, water gurgling over large rocks in the river that curved around the edge of the large flat floor. It was beautiful. Nature's sounds and smells.

Breathe. Enjoy the moment. For today, she was here. In this place. In this particular moment.

It was all good.

Her eyes caught sight of the tents behind her car and her new-found calm abruptly evaporated.

All was good...*except* for the local police sergeant.

When she'd arrived that morning, Jack had proudly shown her the tent he'd set up for her. Another well-prepared person was camping very close. Obviously, a competitor because there was a horse float and a makeshift corral of electric tape. She'd put her bag in on the camp stretcher. Then, and only then, had Jack casually mentioned the tent next to hers belonged to Tom Jamieson.

A wave of chaotic heat swept up from her toes as she remembered the moment.

How was she supposed to avoid the man when she was

practically sleeping with him? Sure, they were separated by thin layers of waterproof nylon.

And a few feet of air.

Hardly any sort of barrier at all. She'd hear him when he moved in his tent, in his sleeping bag.

She swallowed.

He'd hear her.

She'd wanted to demand that Jack dismantle her tent and set it up somewhere else. Preferably on the other side of the river, the other side of the basin.

The other side of Australia! A small snicker of laughter escaped her.

She'd even mumbled some stilted half-sentences about moving but Jack had looked at her as though she'd lost her mind. Little did he know how close he was to being right.

She was powerless to control her physical reaction when Tom Jamieson was near her. The tiny shivers that spiralled out of her stomach to every part of her body, clogging her throat, cramping the function of her lungs. Sending her heart into tachycardia. But she could make damned sure he never guessed the struggle she was having.

Cool.

Calm.

Collected.

Her watchwords for dealing with Tom Jamieson.

A loud equine snort jerked her out of her mental pep talk.

A sudden prickle of awareness shivered across her skin. With a feeling of inevitability, she stopped and turned. At eye level was a black mane on a gleaming brown horse. But more disturbing, a pair of lean moleskin-covered legs astride the large creature. A man's hand held leather reins in a relaxed grip, a second hand rested on the thigh nearest to her, long masculine fingers splayed across taut navy fabric.

She'd been thinking about Tom and now here he was as though she'd conjured him up.

She looked up into his smiling face and her heart did a slow somersault before quivering behind her sternum like a jelly. At this rate she'd need to call the paramedics for defibrillation. Everything about this moment would be imprinted on her memory. The curve of his lips, the creak of the saddle, a pleasant animal mustiness from the sun-warmed horse.

Damn.

She was a city girl. Sales at big department stores made her pulse career out of control. Not moments filled with these earthy scents and sights and sounds.

Nature had an evil sense of humour.

CHAPTER FIVE

'ARE you following me, Sergeant?'

'Tom.'

'Are you following me…Sergeant *Tom*?'

He laughed, the corners of his eyes crinkling attractively. Her traitorous heart gave a quick leap. She set her lips, ruthlessly suppressing the smile that wanted to form. If she wasn't careful, he'd think she was bantering with him, encouraging him. The last thing she needed.

His laughter faded and he leaned confidingly towards her. The fabric of his pale blue chambray shirt pulled at the shoulder, moulding to the muscle beneath. He rested a lean, tanned forearm on the front of the saddle, his hand dangling at eye level. She frowned, resisting the impulse to step back.

His eyes made a leisurely examination of her face and then he said, 'Yes.'

She squinted at him, her mind scrambling to make sense of the word. The small silence snapped at her nerves. 'Yes, what?'

'Yes, I am following you,' he clarified.

'Oh.' Her voice came out as a feeble squeak. She cleared her throat. 'Why?'

'When I saw you heading away from the arena, I guessed you'd be going back to camp for a cuppa.' His voice purred along her auditory pathways as she stared at the small satisfied smile curving his mouth. 'I thought I'd join you.'

'Don't you have things to do? Official duties?' She looked back towards the arena in the hope that a task might materialise for him. 'Judging or something?'

'Not right now.' The warmth in his eyes made her pulse jump. 'And, besides, I wanted to talk to you.'

She took a deep breath and recited her mantra again.

Cool.

Calm.

Collected. Was it too much to ask of her cavorting insides? Apparently, it was, because her heart kept chiselling at her ribcage.

'What did you want to talk to me about?' She managed to fix him with a steady look.

'Anything and everything, Kayla.' There it was again, that lingering verbal caress of her name. 'I enjoy crossing swords with you. There's a certain spice to it that I can't seem to resist. You interest me. I want to know what makes you tick.'

'You must be a very busy man if you're this curious with everyone.' She couldn't prevent the tinge of asperity that had crept into her voice.

'Ah, but I'm not this curious with just anyone.' When he paused, she felt her stomach tighten in anticipation of what he'd say next. 'Only the people I want to know better. Like you.' He gave her a sly smile. 'And members of the criminal fraternity, but that's part of the job.'

A small bubble of laughter escaped catching her by surprise. 'You're a typical policeman, aren't you?'

'I am. Does that bother you?' His gaze sharpened with predatory interest as he straightened in the saddle. The horse shifted restlessly beneath him but Tom didn't take his eyes off hers.

She shrugged. 'Why would it?'

'Tsk. Never answer a question with a question. It's one of

those things that makes us typical policemen suspicious.' His eyes narrowed and she wondered what he read in her face because when she didn't say anything, he murmured, 'Policing is a job, Kayla, not a personality trait.'

'I know that.' She felt oddly raw, unprepared to hear the questions she could see forming in his mind. Marshalling her thoughts, she said, 'You said you wanted to talk to me?'

'I do.' He kicked his feet out of the stirrups and in the next instant he'd landed lightly on the ground beside her.

Impossibly close.

She took a small surreptitious step in retreat as he passed the reins over his mount's head. Holding them loosely in one hand, he turned to face her and swept his arm towards the tents. 'Shall we?'

So much for her escape. She turned and walked beside him. The sooner they got over to Liz and Jack, the sooner Tom's company would be diluted. Surely the impact on her senses would diminish with others around.

But it wasn't to be. When they arrived at the van, it was deserted.

'How about getting the billy on while I put Ziggy away?' He pointed to the neat cooking set up she'd seen earlier. 'Milk's in the esky. Mugs are on the rack. Sugar and teabags in the box.'

'How prosaic,' she murmured. 'You don't throw a scoop of loose tea into the billy with a handful of eucalyptus leaves?'

His lips twitched. 'We can try that another day if you like. For today, teabags are easier. I take mine white with one.'

She nodded and crossed to where a blackened pot with a spout sat on a small portable gas cooker. A peek inside the billy revealed plenty of water so she lit the burner.

Everything was very orderly and in a short time she'd gathered the things she needed. With the water heating, she looked over to where Tom was working beside the float. He had the saddle off Ziggy and was brushing the glossy brown coat. The horse lowered his head and blew loudly through his nostrils. It sounded like a snort of contentment. The care Tom took with the big animal touched her.

Helpless to resist while he had his back to her, she ran her eyes over his frame. The muscles in his broad shoulders rippled and bunched with each long, powerful sweep of his arm. His light shirt followed the contours of his torso as it tapered to his trim waist and narrow hips.

After a few moments, he turned aside to put the brush in a carrier nearby and bent to pick up Ziggy's nearest front foot. The horse turned its head to rest its muzzle on Tom's lumbar region. There was a sweetness and trust in the gesture that brought an unexpected lump to her throat. As Tom worked his way around to each foot, she realised that Ziggy was obligingly lifting each foot for attention. Man and horse were obviously a well-established partnership.

When Tom had finished, he straightened, ran a hand over the horse's haunches then walked across to the corral. Ziggy ambled after him and Kayla realised the animal wasn't tethered. Tom unhitched a section of tape. The horse walked over to a pile of hay on the ground and took a mouthful. After a detour to check the bucket, Tom let himself out of the makeshift yard and turned towards her. His long legs began eating up the short distance between them.

She swallowed and snapped her attention to the cooker in front of her where steam was now rising out of the narrow spout. Glad to have something to do with her hands, she picked up the pot and poured hot water over the teabags she had ready.

In her peripheral vision, she saw Tom open a couple of folding chairs as she added a splash of milk to both brews.

With the teaspoon poised over the sugar, she asked, 'Heaped or flat?'

'Heaped.'

'Need sweetening?' She stirred the liquid.

'Some might say so.' He gave her a lopsided grin then leaned down to pick up the drink. 'Thanks. Grab a seat.'

She lifted her own mug and moved to join him. They relaxed into the chairs and the silence between them stretched. To her surprise, it was undemanding, almost comfortable. Sounds around them filled the void. Ziggy's steady munching, the clip-clop of hooves as a competitor trotted past, lowing of cattle. An empty stock truck clattered through the grounds to the other side of the arena.

'I saw you arrive this morning,' Tom said.

'Did you?' She blew on her steaming drink and took a small sip.

'Of course. I'm a policeman. We notice things.'

'Ah, yes.' Thank goodness he hadn't been at the tents to see her reaction to the camping arrangements. She hated to think what conclusions he might have drawn from her appalled expression.

'What do you think of the camp draft?'

She sent him a sideways glance under her lashes and, tongue firmly in cheek, she said, 'As far as I can see, it's a glorified excuse to chase around after a cow.'

'Bite your tongue.' He laughed and the sound rolled over her deliciously. 'It's not a cow. It's called a *beast.*'

'So I've been told.'

'And we don't *chase around* after it, we *control* it.'

'Mmm, control. I understand.' She nodded. 'So camp drafting is a sport for men who like to control things?'

'Hardly,' he said with a chuckle. 'Half a ton of beef on the hoof can be a tad stroppy.' He took a sip of tea. 'As for being in control—who doesn't like things to go their way?'

'True. Very true.' She looked down at the scuffed toes on her boots and contemplated that she was enjoying being here with him, just talking. Her system had started to settle. Her heart no longer thrummed in the desperate, unsustainable beat that felt like it would break out of her ribcage. Now it was a more pleasant, alive feeling. A hum of vitality and energy. Perhaps she'd been tackling the issue of Tom Jamieson all wrong. Maybe she needed to stop avoiding him and see *more* of him instead. Desensitise herself with small doses often.

She turned the option over in her mind, examining it for flaws.

'For instance,' he said breaking into her thoughts, 'I'd like to understand why you react to me the way you do.'

Her stomach dipped as she eyed him warily. So much for enjoying the conversation. She had a feeling he was about to prod her back out of her complacent thoughts.

When she didn't say anything he tilted his head to one side and contemplated her. 'At first, I wondered if it was because you didn't like me.' He didn't sound annoyed, just... meditative.

'Did you?' She took another quick sip to moisten her suddenly parched mouth.

He swirled his mug and stared into it as though an answer might be hidden in the hot tea. 'But then I decided that couldn't be the case.'

'You—you did?' She was unwillingly curious.

He lifted his eyes to focus on her; intelligence gleamed in his piercing look. He nodded slowly. 'I realised you don't know me well enough to dislike me.'

'Oh.' Not a question, but definitely something that required an answer of some sort. She fingered the handle of her mug as she debated what to say. After a moment, she slid a look at him. 'Does that mean if I get to know you, it will be okay to dislike you then?'

He grinned his appreciation at the way she'd evaded a direct comment. 'No, that's not what I mean at all. *When*, not *if*, you get to know me, I'm sure you'll be charmed by my wit and sparkling personality.'

'And your modesty. Don't forget that.' Her biggest problem was that with his humorous approach he *was* charming her.

'You bet. Faint hearts and fair ladies.' He paused for a moment. 'Would you agree you're an open-minded person, Kayla? The sort who judges people on their merits?'

'I try to be.' But she knew she hadn't been fair with him. She had a feeling he was about to call her on it.

'Then why have you been giving me the cold shoulder?'

'*Trying* to give you the cold shoulder,' she corrected, with a rueful smile. 'I've been spectacularly unsuccessful.'

His lips twitched but other than that she could see he was waiting for an answer. She sighed. She'd give him one, but it wasn't a good one.

'It seemed the best way of handling you.'

'Why?' he asked softly.

'It's the way I deal with the unknown. I keep it at a distance.'

'I've seen you meeting Jack and Liz's other friends for the first time. No sign of frost then. Only when I'm around.'

So it hadn't been her imagination. He had watched her at the social events. She rolled the body of her mug between her hands. His perception was unsettling. 'That's what I mean. *You* are the unknown. You're not my...type.'

'What type am I?'

Sexy, dangerous, masculine, threatening? Overwhelming? Larger than life? Much more man than she could handle? Impossible words and phrases paraded through her mind. She couldn't say any of them. 'Large. Dominant. In the police force.'

'That's the third time you've brought up my job. Interesting. You don't seem the sort who'd have run foul of the law to build up that sort of prejudice.' She waited for him to draw the inevitable conclusion. 'So maybe your experience is a more personal one.'

Her hands were suddenly clammy against the stainless

steel of the mug. She tried to think of something to change the subject.

'Someone you went out with?'

'Yes,' she said reluctantly.

'Close?'

She tightened her fingers around the mug. 'We were engaged.'

'Past tense.' After a moment he added, 'But perhaps not very past tense.'

'No, not very.'

'I'm sorry,' he said softly, and tears prickled at the backs of her eyes. She'd thought she was all cried out over Keith. She *was* all cried out—it was Tom's sympathy that was undoing her.

'Don't be.' Her voice was husky with the choky feeling in her throat. 'It was for the best.'

'How long before you came up here?'

'A couple of months.'

'Rough?'

'Yes, it was at the time.'

'Tell me his name. I have connections. I'll have him busted to constable.'

She laughed despite herself, grateful to him for lightening the moment so her incipient tears could recede. 'Tempting, but not a good idea. Besides...I think his connections are better.'

'Really?'

'Mmm.' She pursed her mouth then told him the rest. 'He was marrying his boss's daughter.'

'His boss's daughter?' He sounded thoughtful. 'Using my superior powers of deduction, I'll take a stab and say your father's in the police force.'

'Impressive, Sherlock.'

'I think I can do better. Morgan? That wouldn't be Assistant Commissioner Christopher Morgan, would it?'

'It would.'

She held her breath, waiting for his reaction. Would he be overawed by her father's rank, the way Keith had? Would he see her as a way to fast-track his career?

Tom was silent for a long moment and then he laughed—a genuine sound. 'Yeah, I guess his connections are better. Still, he must have blotted his copybook with your father when you broke it off.'

'Not really.' The support from such an unlikely source pierced straight to her heart. The truth was, far from Tom's assumption, her father thought she was a feather-brained female by breaking it off with his rising star. Now Tom, a man she hardly knew, was standing in her corner. No questions asked.

She'd been a convenience for Keith—one that had become inconvenient when she'd confided in him about her brother-in-law's pass. Even in private, he hadn't been able to be a rock in her time of need.

'Your dad took his side?'

'My father didn't know the whole story behind the break-up.'

'And you think that's okay?'

'Not okay.' She shrugged. 'But unless he knew all the facts, how could he make a decision about whose side to take?'

'You're his daughter, his family. His allegiance should be automatic.'

Should it? It hadn't ever worked that way in her family. She was silent for a long moment. 'You are a nice man, Tom Jamieson.'

He made a hissing sound of disgust through his teeth. *'Nice?'* His mouth curved and his eyes glinted with humour. 'Well, it's a long way from charming but it's a start.'

A small snort of laughter escaped. She bit her lip to smother the unfamiliar sound.

Looking pleased with himself, Tom stretched his legs out in

front of him and crossed them at the ankles. She swallowed, all desire to laugh instantly subsiding.

'What were your other two objections to me? Large and dominant?' Tom asked. 'I can't do anything about *large* except to say I would never hurt you physically, Kayla. Never.'

There was nothing but truth in his warm brown eyes. She ducked her head. 'I believe you.'

'Then that just leaves dominant. Is that such a problem? You're pretty bossy yourself. You didn't have any trouble telling me what to do at Andy's accident. Or ignoring what I wanted you to do.'

He was whittling away her objections, gently, thoroughly, leaving her naked, without protection.

'You wouldn't want a marshmallow man.' He sat forward again, his voice pitched low and intimate. 'You'd walk all over him.'

She stood and walked to the kitchen set up to relight the billy. She had to do something with her hands and making a second cup of tea seemed as good as anything. 'Did you want another cup of tea?'

'No, but I would like you to stop avoiding me, Kayla.'

She turned back to face him. 'I'm not sure where you're going with this. I've agreed that you're nicer than I expected. I'll even admit to the possibility that a warm, sparkling personality might lurk behind your rugged, law-enforcement-officer exterior. What more can I do?'

'Come to my family's barbecue tonight. We always get together on the Saturday night of the camp draft weekend.'

She shook her head. 'I can't gatecrash a family tradition, and besides, I'm here with Liz and Jack.'

'They'll be there. All comers are welcome. There's nothing exclusive about a Jamieson get-together. You'd have ended up coming across with them anyway.'

'Oh.'

He walked across and put his empty mug into the wash bucket. 'This just means you'll be there with me.'

'Then I suppose it would be okay. Where is it?'

His mouth twitched. 'Over the other side of the arena.'

'Okay.' She lifted the lid on the teabag container and got one out. 'Liz and Jack will know.'

'They do.' He looked down at her and said softly, 'But make no mistake here, Kayla. I'm asking you to come with *me*, so I'll come and pick you up.'

'But it'd be just as easy for me to walk over with them, wouldn't it?'

'A gentleman always picks up his date from her front door,' he said lightly.

She scowled. 'It's a tent.'

'From her tent flap, then.' He grinned. 'I want you to walk over with me, Kayla.'

'Oh, very well.' With fumbling fingers, she fitted the lid onto the canister. Picking the container up, she clutched it to her chest like a shield and turned to face him. '*But* since you're so insistent on that, I have some demands of my own.'

His eyelids drooped slightly, giving him a deceptive, sleepy look that was belied by the slow, sexy smile that touched his lips. 'Tell me your demands and I'll do my best to satisfy them.'

Her heart kicked hard and scalding heat crawled up her neck, cell by cell, into her face. *God, what did he think she'd meant?* She longed to bring her hands up, press them to her cheeks, hide them from his gaze. Her fingers tightened on the canister, the plastic lip digging into her palm.

'Ground rules,' she blurted. 'I mean I want to set ground rules.'

His smile faded. 'Ground rules?'

'No…funny business. Strictly friends.' Marvellous. She sounded as gauche as a teen going on her first date.

'Of course.' He nodded gravely, his eyes guileless as they held hers. 'Best behaviour. Nothing you don't approve of.'

'Just as long as we're clear.' She tried hard to concentrate on his words, feeling there was a trap there but not able to concentrate her mind to identify it.

'Crystal clear. Don't look so worried. It'll all work out, you'll see.' He grinned, a natural friendly expression not loaded with innuendo this time. She wondered if she'd misjudged him earlier. 'I'd better get back to the arena to help out.' He lifted his hand and stroked her cheek. 'I'll see you later.'

'Okay. Yes. Good. See you.' The skin on her cheek tingled from his tiny caress.

She watched him walk away, her eyes straying over the broad shoulders and straight back, the long legs. Her physical and emotional reactions mocked her. Clammy hands, racing pulse, abdominal gymnastics. How could she ever think she could desensitise herself against someone like him?

He was a sexy man with a brand of masculinity her feminine weakness yearned towards.

Blast him.

She had to shore up her defences, try to contain her vulnerability. She was only here for another four months. Too short to explore anything even if she wanted to. Not that he'd asked her to... She had to remember, she had plans. Places to go, things to do. A rebellion and a search for herself as much as anything.

Nothing that involved Tom Jamieson.

Nothing that involved *any* man.

Tom wanted to gentle her as he would one of his young foals, imprint her with the idea that he was someone she could trust, that he was someone she could let close, someone who wouldn't betray her. Or ask more than she could give.

But maybe he was lying to himself...wasn't he already

asking more than she wanted to give? She wanted to deny the chemistry between them and her defences were well honed.

He'd made steps this morning, dispelled much of the chill between them but none of the sexual tension. Her astringent sense of humour had him on his toes to keep up with her. She was an interesting combination of good humour and vulnerability when she relaxed her guard.

Liz had been right when she'd warned him that Kayla had been hurt. Tom clenched his jaw, feeling his teeth grind under the pressure. The men in her life obviously hadn't appreciated her special blend of strength and sensitivity and honour.

Assistant Commissioner Morgan was her father. Hard to imagine him being a parent. Must have been tough, being his kid. The man was a straight arrow, incorruptible, uncompromising and well-known throughout the force for his rigid, by-the-book approach to everything. For his job that approach was commendable.

For raising a daughter...perhaps not quite so good. How did a child respond to that sort of environment? Perfectionism? Self-reliance? There was a key to understanding Kayla.

And he really, really wanted to understand her.

He remembered her flushed face when she'd been laying down the law about tonight. Clutching those teabags in front of her like some sort of talisman to ward off invaders. He had no problems with her ground rules.

Not that it would stop him from prodding at the boundaries. But he'd always respect her. She had nothing to worry about.

For now.

He'd worked with horses all his life and had a horseman's appreciation for the finer details of the chase. Of when to apply pressure to a wary creature and when to back off to get a filly to come to him willingly.

But once she did, she was going to be his.

CHAPTER SIX

BACK at the arena, Kayla sat on one of the folding chairs in front of the first-aid tent and listened to the commentator announce the scores.

The latest young competitor had had a disappointing run and now his beast trotted in brief, glorious freedom around the edge of the arena. Mounted attendants converged on the animal to usher it efficiently towards the race at the other end of the enclosure.

Kayla swept her gaze over the riders absentmindedly and then continued to scan the area. A fizz of dismay and resignation rippled through her stomach as she realised she was searching for a *particular* tall, lean figure.

Tom Jamieson.

God, what was wrong with her? Tom wasn't around—she should be *glad*, not trying to find him. Sure, they'd talked, settled some of her wariness. But that didn't make them best buddies. And it was certainly no reason to be visually stalking him like a...camp draft groupie—if there was such a thing. The cup of tea they'd had together had been pleasant... fun, even...but it still didn't mean she was going to seek him out.

Tom had said he enjoyed crossing swords with her. She was honest enough to admit there was a perverse enjoyment in their tension-riddled contact. As though she was flying too close to the sun, flirting with something perilous yet irresistible.

Though, to be fair, he hadn't put a foot wrong. It was the way he made her feel inside. He didn't have to do anything—just be himself. That aura of reckless danger radiated from him.

In her heart, she knew she was no match for him. The courage it would take to keep up with a man like Tom Jamieson was beyond her grasp.

She stood and moved restlessly around the tent, running a distracted eye over the supplies.

A burst of static from the loudspeaker system cut into her. 'The last rider into camp before we break for lunch is Ryan Collins on Misty Lady.'

A collective gasp from the people on the small spectator stand nearby drew her attention back to the arena. She crossed to the fence as the stewards opened the double gates. A brown and white steer burst out of the camp, closely pursued by a slender rider on a grey horse. The fearless boy seemed younger than the thirteen she knew he must be to compete in the camp draft. Lanky, with an uncoordinated look, the way his arms were pumping to urge his horse to go faster.

Unimpressed, the steer began to duck and weave, looking for a way to escape. Kayla's heart leapt to her throat as the horse plunged to the side. The sudden move caught the rider by surprise and she could see his frantic grab for the saddle. For a moment she thought he might recover but in the next second he was tumbling, all long legs and arms, to land, hands first on the sandy surface. Kayla darted back to the tent to grab the medical kit.

Her eyes fixed on the still, sprawled figure in the centre of the arena, she dashed towards the nearest gate. One of the spectators had it open for her.

'Thanks.' She threw the word over her shoulder as she ran.

A man vaulted the fence further around the perimeter and in a dozen strides was beside the now-struggling child.

Tom.

Tossing his hat carelessly to the ground, he sank to his knees and reached out to help.

By the time she took her last few steps, the boy was sitting up and cradled against Tom's bigger, stronger body.

'M-my arm hurts.' The boy struggled to suppress his sobs but the tear tracks streaked through the dust on his pale cheeks. He clutched his arm to his body, his face screwed up with pain.

'I know, Ryan,' Tom said, his voice gravelly with sympathy. 'Here's the doc to patch you up.'

The boy's moisture-drenched dark brown eyes blinked at her warily.

'Hey, Ryan. I'm Kayla,' she said as she knelt beside the pair, noting Tom's tender, supporting embrace. His eyes, when she met them briefly, mirrored Ryan's anguish.

Turning her attention back to her patient, she said 'Let's have a look at what you've done to yourself, shall we?'

'It hurts t-too much.' He hunched away, curling his face into Tom's shoulder, protective of the injured limb and wanting to prevent her from touching it. 'Uncle Tom?' The plea stark with fear.

Uncle Tom? Suddenly the family resemblance between the two was obvious—those thickly lashed, deep brown eyes, the wavy, nearly black hair. Ryan was the spitting image of how a young Tom must have looked.

'Ry, you need—' Tom began in a tortured voice.

'It's okay,' Kayla interrupted gently, touching Tom on the hand as she addressed Ryan. 'We can have a look at the rest of you for a minute, can't we, Ryan? Is your arm the only bit that hurts?'

He nodded, still huddling into Tom. 'I th-think so.'

'What about your head? Did you hit it when you landed?'

'N-no.'

'That's good.' She smiled at him. 'Will you let me undo your helmet for you?'

He uncurled a little and tilted his head so she could reach the chin buckle. She gently removed the protective cap.

'I'm just going to touch your neck and back. I want you to tell me if anything hurts. Can you do that?'

'Y-yes.' Some of the tension eased across Ryan's shoulders now that he realised she wasn't going to insist on handling his arm immediately.

Kayla pressed gently down his slender neck. 'How's that feel?'

'O-okay.'

'And here? Any pain?' she asked. She worked around his shoulders and upper arms, acutely aware of the way Tom shifted his grip on his nephew, anticipating her moves, making it easier for her to continue her examination.

'No. It feels okay,' said Ryan.

'Good.' She sat back on her heels and kept a hand on his shoulder as she did a visual assessment of his cradled arm. There was swelling, which meant the delicate bones at his wrist were obscured compared to his uninjured arm. But no blood, no obvious bone displacement, good colour in his fingertips. All positive signs. 'Tell me about the pain in your arm. If I said ten was really, really bad and one was hardly hurting at all, how does yours feel?'

'M-maybe an eight. Or—or a nine. B-but I don't want an injection.'

'No injections.' She met Tom's eyes briefly in silent communication before looking back at Ryan. 'Do you have any medical problems, Ryan? Asthma? Anything else? Do you take any medicine regularly?'

The boy shook his head.

'He's as fit as a fiddle,' Tom said, reading her message and adding his confirmation to Ryan's silent answer. 'But you're a bit accident-prone, aren't you, matey?'

'Yeah.' A faint sheepish grin creased Ryan's drawn face. 'That's what Mum says, too.'

'Great. I have something that will help with the pain before we take a look at your arm.' She dug out an inhaler and quickly charged it with liquid analgesic. 'You need to pop the end in your mouth and suck air through it.'

She read the child's reluctance to let go of his injured limb. 'How about we get your uncle to hold that for you? You just use it whenever you need to.'

Tom adjusted his support of his nephew so he could take the assembled unit. The murmur of the crowd filtered into her consciousness while she waited for the boy to take a couple of good, deep breaths.

'Ryan, I'm just going to take your pulse on your sore arm and then touch your fingers, is that okay? We won't move it yet. I promise.'

'Okay.' Ryan sucked hard on the inhaler and his eyes followed her movements as she curled her fingers carefully around his wrist to feel for the radial pulse. As she expected, the beat was strong and steady, if a little rapid.

Lightly running her fingers over each of his digits, she said, 'Can you feel me doing that?'

'Yes.'

She turned to the kit, located the inflatable splints and chose the size she needed. 'We need to put a splint on your arm to hold your bones still, Ryan. It'll help with your pain. This is what we'll use.' She showed Ryan the opening. 'See, it's a tube. I'll slip your arm in and then I can pump it full of air until it's a nice, firm bubble. Can I do that for you now?'

The boy bit his lip, looking up at the man holding him for guidance. A lump formed in Kayla's throat at the naked

affection in Tom's face as he gave Ryan a smiling nod. With
the encouragement, her young patient took a deep breath, tears
springing to his eyes as he said, 'Okay.'

'You're being very brave.'

'Thanks.' Ryan hiccupped then said, 'It was pretty dumb,
though, huh, Uncle Tom? Falling off like that.'

'Nah, happens to all of us, Ry,' Tom said. 'You've seen me
come a cropper. Remember when Ziggy bucked me off in the
ditch?'

Kayla slid the splint over Ryan's hand and carefully worked
it along his forearm as Tom talked.

'Y-yeah, you stunk,' said Ryan with a watery chuckle.

'What happened?' Kayla asked.

'Uncle Tom landed head first in the water.' Ryan wiped
his cheek with the palm of his uninjured hand, smearing the
dust and moisture into a muddy smut.

'Yeah. I was putrid, wasn't I? Even after I showered, the
smell stayed in my nose.'

'M-mum wouldn't let him come inside until he'd hosed
off.'

'Which wouldn't have been so bad, except it was the middle
of winter and the water was cold.'

'Poor Uncle Tom.' Kayla smiled at Ryan before she flicked
a glance at Tom.

His answering smile promised retribution. 'I can tell how
sorry you feel for me.'

'Oh, I do.' She swallowed and made the final tweak to
position the splint.

'At least, y-you didn't cry or anything.' Ryan must have
suddenly compared his uncle's accident and the aftermath to
his own performance and found himself wanting. His voice
was unsteady again as he said, 'D-don't tell Hannah that I
bawled, will you?'

Kayla squeezed the bulb of the splint pump and air began to fill the clear plastic sleeve.

'I won't.'

'Promise? Only g-girls cry,' Ryan said as he watched the splint inflate. 'I d-don't want everyone to know.'

'It's okay to cry, Ryan,' Kayla said gently. The boy gave her such a look of horrified disbelief that she bit the inside of her cheek to stop herself from chuckling. 'It's true. No one should be ashamed to have a good cry if they need to.' She flashed a pointed glance at the tall man cradling the boy. 'Should they…Uncle Tom?'

His amusement was clear in the twitch of his mouth. 'Kayla's right, Ry,' he said to his nephew, but his warm brown eyes lingered on hers.

With an effort, she dragged her gaze away and checked the firmness of the air splint.

'*You* don't cry,' Ryan said, twisting his head so he could look up into the man's face.

'I don't cry where you can see me, kiddo,' Tom said softly. 'There's a difference.'

Kayla's heart melted as he surprised her yet again with his sensitivity. She'd expected him to mouth a quick platitude. Instead, his answer was meaningful, filled with a touching honesty and a wealth of personal experience behind the admission. *What would bring a man like Tom Jamieson to the point of tears?*

'How's your pain level now, Ryan?' she said, pulling her attention back to her patient.

'Better. Yeah.'

'Good. Let's fix you up with this sling,' she said, threading a fabric triangle under his arm then leaning forward so she could tie the ends at the back of his neck. 'I'll organise a stretcher and we can get you out of here.'

'I can walk.'

'But you're—'

'I want to. Please.' His eyes beseeched her before turning to Tom.

'I'll help him, Kayla,' Tom said softly. 'He'll be okay.'

She pursed her lips for a moment then nodded. Both male faces lit up with identical expressions of relief. Suppressing the urge to shake her head at them, she closed up the medical kit. Hoisting the strap onto her shoulder, she stood by ready to assist, but Tom had everything under control. He braced Ryan with loving care and got the boy to his feet. Ryan straightened and Kayla scrutinised her patient's face.

'How do you feel?' she said. 'Not light-headed? Sick?'

'No. I'm good.' Ryan squared his shoulders and stepped forward. On either side of him, she and Tom hovered like anxious guardians, matching his pace.

A cheer went up from the crowd. Ryan's pale cheeks flushed with quiet pride as he lifted a hand in acknowledgement.

Ten minutes later, Tom had Kayla and Ryan tucked into the back seat of his four-wheel drive and was heading for Dustin.

At the intersection, he braked and turned his head to check his precious cargo. Kayla's head was bent towards his nephew, a swing of straight golden hair hiding her profile. She reached up and brushed it back, tucking it behind her ear as he'd seen her do often. She was smiling at Ryan. Her body was curved towards the boy, ready to anticipate his needs. She adjusted the seat belt for him and murmured something. Ryan looked up and smiled. The trust in his nephew's expression made Tom's chest tighten.

He cleared his throat. 'Everything okay back there?'

'Yes,' two voices chorused. Kayla lifted soft grey eyes to meet his.

Tom faced the front again, checked the way was clear then pulled out onto the road.

'Uncle Tom?'

'Yes, Ry?'

'Mum's on duty this morning. Will she look after me?'

'Probably. I've spoken to her so she knows we're on the way.' He glanced at Ryan in the rear-vision mirror then across to Kayla. 'My sister, Ryan's mum, is Charlotte Collins.'

'The radiographer?'

'Yep.'

'Will I have one of those plasters that everyone can sign?' Ryan said, sounding hopeful.

'You will.' Humour laced Kayla's voice.

'Cool. That's better than David. He only had a sling when he broke his collarbone.' There was a small silence. When Tom looked up again, Ryan was yawning. 'When will I be able to ride again?'

'Well, let's get you fixed up before we say for sure,' Kayla said, gently. 'You'll need the plaster on for six weeks and then we'll see. How is your pain now?'

'Okay. I'm tired,' he mumbled through another yawn.

'Why don't you close your eyes?'

A few minutes later, Tom glanced up to see Kayla had her arm around Ryan. His nephew's head rested on her shoulder.

Tom swallowed hard. The picture sent a shaft of pure emotion arrowing so strongly to his heart, it bordered on pain.

She'd handled his nephew flawlessly in the arena, no frustration with his reluctance to have her examine his arm. Just a smooth segue into other checks until Ryan had the confidence to let her near the painful injury. She was fantastic to have around, taking charge, easing difficult moments in an emergency.

He loved the way she'd been so sensitive, quickly grasping Ryan's need to walk out of the arena on his own two feet. Tom had been able to tell she hadn't been happy about it, but she'd understood it was important.

He liked working with her. They made a good team.

A damned good team.

An achy warmth expanded through his chest. The more he knew Kayla, the more he wanted to know.

As Kayla had expected, Ryan's arm had a classic greenstick fracture. A minor manipulation while he was under heavy sedation reduced it. And then she'd put a cast on his forearm.

Now back in the care of his mother, Ryan had immediately tried to extract a promise from the frazzled woman that she'd take him back out for the camp draft barbecue as planned.

'Maybe. We'll see how you are in a couple of hours,' Charlotte prevaricated.

'We'd better head back out to the flat, Charlie,' Tom said with a glance at his watch.

'Of course.' Charlotte turned to Kayla. 'Thank you both again for looking after Ryan.'

'No problem, Charlotte. Everything should be fine with his arm now but let me know if you have any concerns,' Kayla said.

'I will, thank you.' Charlotte put her arm across her son's shoulders and he snuggled into her side without any self-consciousness. 'Good luck, Tom. And listen, I don't want to see you in here later.'

Tom grinned. 'Yes, boss. See you, Ry.'

'Let's go, Kayla.' He took her arm and Kayla was aware of Charlotte's eyes darting between them curiously.

'Sure. Bye, Ryan, Charlotte.'

Tom shifted his hand to the small of her back and the warmth of his touch through the light cotton of her shirt was all she could think of until he was holding the door of his vehicle open for her.

She clambered into the front passenger seat and watched him walk around the bonnet to the driver's door. His sister's parting words suddenly popped into her mind.

'Why did Charlotte wish you luck?'

'For this afternoon,' he said as he reversed out of the parking space.

Oh. God. She swallowed. 'You're competing in the camp draft?'

'Of course.' He put the car in gear and spun the steering-wheel. 'Are you going to watch?'

'No!'

He glanced at her, raising his eyebrows at her instinctive response.

'I…don't know,' she said, moderating her tone. 'Maybe.' Her heart lurched. *Probably.*

'In medieval times, you'd have given me a token to wear to show your allegiance.'

'Would I?' she said dryly. 'Wouldn't that depend?'

'On?'

'On whether I…um…favoured you.'

'And do you?' His voice flowed like honey over her, leaving heat sweeping through her.

Oh, heavens. Too much, too fast. Too terrifying.

'Well, I certainly don't want to see you skewered on the end of a lance or a cow horn, if that's what you mean.'

'Chicken.' He laughed. 'You're dodging the issue.'

'Not at all,' she said smoothly. 'Back in medieval times, I'd only have to boil a few newts' eyes in my cauldron. Whether you got well or not would have been foretold in the entrails of some poor unsuspecting chicken. These days, it's my job to stitch up any messy aftermaths.'

'Speaking of aftermaths,' he said, his voice soft and sincere, 'you were wonderful with Ryan today. Thank you.'

'He was a trouper.'

They spent the rest of the short journey chatting companionably. She had the feeling Tom was *managing* her, dictating the tenor of their conversations. A little push here, a relaxing topic there.

It had to be her imagination—why would he bother?

'I'll see you shortly,' Tom said as he dropped her at the arena.

'Sure.'

She walked slowly over to the stands, casting a brief look over her shoulder to see him driving slowly over to their camp. He was going to pick up Ziggy so they could compete. She still wasn't sure if she wanted to watch, but how could she not?

As each successive competitor was announced, she felt sick with apprehension until she knew it wasn't Tom's turn.

'Next in camp is Tom Jamieson.'

Her heart froze.

She watched as Tom and Ziggy ambled into the penned area and stood relaxed at the end for a signal from the judge.

Tom looked over at her and winked, his teeth a flash of white in his face. Her fingers curled into fists and she held them tight in her lap. She was relieved to see that, like all the riders before him, he wore a helmet.

With his back leg cocked, Ziggy stood looking half-asleep. Tom was running his eyes over the cattle at the other end of the fenced area. Kayla knew enough now to know he was choosing his beast. She glanced at the small milling herd, wondering which one looked most cooperative. They all looked the same—large and black with broad, wet noses and big, suspicious eyes.

'Okay,' said the judge.

Tom straightened, gathering the reins. Ziggy's demeanour changed instantly, his ears flickering back and forth. Tom's eyes focussed and he moved forward. Still relaxed but with obvious intent. Almost stalking.

Ziggy's step had a controlled spring and the horse seemed to know which of the animals Tom had chosen.

Slowly, slowly, Tom and Ziggy rode through the group. There was no panic, they seemed to just be moseying around.

And then, suddenly, one of the beasts was free at the gate end of the camp, separated from the others by Tom and Ziggy.

In a desperate attempt to rejoin its herd, the beast tried to bolt along the fence.

But Ziggy was ready. The big horse dived at the wooden barrier, cutting off escape.

Kayla gasped, pressing her clenched fists against her mouth, mashing her lips against her teeth. Surely Tom would be flung off against the rails. But, no, he and Ziggy worked in a fluid dance as the beast dodged and weaved. There was no way they were going to let the animal evade them. Backwards and forwards. Backwards and forwards. Kayla realised her feet were shuffling in an effort to help.

'Gate.' Tom's voice clipped out the command.

The attendants flung open the double gates at the front of the camp.

The beast charged through with Ziggy in hot pursuit.

Side by side, they rounded the first peg. Man and horse slowed, changed sides to manoeuvre the beast into position for the second peg. And then a huge spurt of speed. Sand flung up from Ziggy's hooves as he curved the animal into the run for the second peg.

Right, right, right.

The horse's shoulder nudged the animal along the desired path. Kayla's heart pounded in her throat. For a moment it seemed as though the beast would resist. And then a yield. The figure eight was completed at a flat gallop.

Down the centre of the arena.

A final turn.

And then through the gate.

The whistle sounded and Kayla leapt to her feet to join with the applause.

A perfect run.

As the excitement of the moment drained away, Kayla realised her joints felt like cooked noodles.

Just as well there was nothing between her and Tom. Or she'd have to give the man a piece of her mind. How dared he scare her like this? Treat his life with so little regard?

CHAPTER SEVEN

'So what's with you and Tom?' Liz's voice floated into the tiny caravan bathroom where Kayla was freshening up for the barbecue.

Her hand jerked and a thick black smudge of mascara appeared on her cheekbone. She softly huffed out a breath and twitched a tissue from the box.

'Nothing.' Using a dab of face cream on the tissue, she scrubbed her skin clean. 'There's nothing with us.'

'But he asked you to the barbecue with his family.'

Kayla's stomach lurched. 'Isn't it like an open house?'

She stared her reflection with dismay. The pink-cheeked woman staring back from the mirror looked…excited, radiant.

Brimming with expectation…but for *what*? This wasn't a real date—it was more of a truce.

She took a deep breath down into her diaphragm to still the swooping sensation. *All comers welcome*, that's what Tom had said.

'Well, yes, it is,' Liz said.

Relief tinged with something less well-defined flashed through Kayla.

Liz went on, 'But he's coming back to pick you up, not entrusting you to Jack and me for directions.' There was a small silence. 'That seems significant.'

'He probably has to come back to get ready anyway since his gear's here.' But if that was the case, wouldn't he already be here?

Significant. Kayla closed her eyes. Tom had called it a date but she'd avoided thinking of it that way. Having Liz attach importance to it gave unwanted weight to his interpretation. She took another deep breath then jammed her few toiletries back in the bag.

'Thanks for the loan of your bathroom,' she said, changing the subject as she clicked the door shut behind her.

'You're very welcome.' Liz sat on the bed with her feet up, one hand rubbing the mound of her stomach.

Concerned, Kayla frowned at her friend. 'Are you okay? Not having pains, are you?'

'No, nothing like that.' Liz sighed. 'I just feel like I've been pregnant for ever and I can't believe there's only one baby in here. It's starting to feel like I'm going to give birth to a teenager.' Her bottom lip pouted for a moment and she wriggled her bare toes. 'And my feet are sore.'

Kayla sat on the end of the bed. 'Poor thing. Shall I give you a foot massage?'

'That wasn't a hint. Really. But...' Liz said, then moaned as Kayla worked her thumb into the arch of one foot. 'Oh, I'll take it. Thank you.'

'Do you think the baby might come early again?'

'Yes.' Then she sighed. 'But maybe it's just wishful thinking. And for goodness' sake, please don't tell Jack or he'll bundle me home and tie me to the bed.'

'Sounds like it has possibilities.'

A strangled snort of laughter spluttered out of Liz. 'Not in my current state but...maybe down the track.' She sighed blissfully as Kayla moved to the other foot. 'Thanks. I was feeling sorry for myself.'

'You should take it easy.'

'Maybe. Kayla...about you and Tom...' Liz trailed off.

'There is no *me and Tom*, so whatever you're worried about, stop it,' Kayla said gently, as she concentrated on the ball of Liz's foot.

'Okay, but I just wanted to say that Tom really is a darling.'

'I'm starting to realise that the sergeant's rugged, manly exterior hides a certain brusque charm.' Kayla eased Liz's feet back on the bed then stood.

As she walked towards the bathroom to wash her hands, she heard Liz getting up.

'It does. He's got a heart of gold,' Liz called as she went down to the kitchen area. 'And you'll like his family. His parents are lovely.'

Kayla's hands froze for the tiniest second on the bar of soap. *Tom's parents.* Her tension ratcheted up a notch. Well, of course they'd be there tonight. He'd said it was a *family* barbecue. Had he considered that when he'd manoeuvred her into this date? She had to believe that he had, so what did that mean, if anything?

She hung up the towel and stepped into the doorway to the kitchen as there was a commotion at the door. Jack poked his head into the van. Two-year-old Emma clung to his neck, all big brown eyes and a froth of glossy brunette ringlets.

He pursed his lips and let out a shrill wolf whistle. 'Two hot babes. What do you think, Emmie?' He grinned at his daughter. 'Your dad is the luckiest man on Welshman's Flat this weekend.'

'Luck-ee.' Emma touched his face.

'Just the usual *babe* for you, darling,' drawled Liz. 'The *hot* one is waiting for Tom.'

Kayla's gut did another quick roll.

'Is that right?' Jack's blue eyes swung back to her. 'Well, well.'

She gritted her teeth, willed her cheeks not to flood with

hot colour and waited for Jack to comment about Tom coming to collect her.

Thankfully, his gaze shifted again to Liz and softened. 'I'll just have to make do with the most beautiful woman in the world.' He flashed his wife a cocky grin and waggled his eyebrows.

'Smooth, very smooth, Jack Campbell.'

Love shone out of every teasing word between Liz and Jack, every heated glance they exchanged. More than love, they truly *liked* each other.

An extraordinary kaleidoscope of truths held Kayla motionless for a moment. Things she'd known intellectually suddenly seemed to reach a visceral level of believability.

Marriage could work.

A large, strong man *didn't* always rule his family with a cold, hard fist.

He didn't have to be regimented to the exclusion of affection.

A large strong man could be sensitive, caring...

Like Jack with Liz and Emma.

She swallowed.

Like Tom had been that morning with Ryan.

Remembering the way he'd cradled his nephew, empathy etched on his face, love clear in the tender way he'd handled his injured nephew. No question of leaving the care of the child to others, he'd been right there, taking care of transport, waiting at the hospital to make sure everything had gone smoothly.

Her chest tightened uncomfortably. He was so different from the men in her family, her father and her brother-in-law. Tom was brave and honest about his softer emotions.

Oh, God, he was more honest than she was. With her background, she felt ill equipped to deal with a man like that.

'What time is Tom coming to pick you up?' Liz's question pulled Kayla out of her reverie.

'About six.' She glanced at her watch. 'Are you ready to go now?'

'Just about.' Liz turned to her husband. 'Darling, I need you to grab some things for Emma.'

'Sure.' He stepped up into the van.

'Let me get out of the way,' Kayla said, moving along the narrow kitchen area.

As Jack made room for her to pass, Emma leaned out from her position in her father's hold, her little arms wide, confident of her welcome. 'Kay-lah. Hold Emmie.'

Kayla stopped to slip her feet back into the boots she'd left at the door. 'Want me to take her while you get the gear?'

'Yeah, thanks.' Jack passed his daughter across.

Kayla took the toddler, settling the child's weight on one hip as she negotiated the steps to the ground outside.

'You're going to have a little brother soon, Emma,' she said, twirling gently. 'What do you think about that?'

'Good. I help,' said Emma and smiled.

'I'll bet you'll be a big help.' Helpless to do anything else, Kayla grinned back at the girl. Her heart filled with a deep, unexpected yearning. 'You know, if I spend too much time with you, I'm going to end up clucky.'

'Cluck-ee.'

'That's right.'

Voluptuous chuckles gurgled in Emma's throat. 'Kay-lah. Cluck-ee.'

'Uh-oh,' she said ruefully at the word association. 'I think I might regret this. How about we find you a different word to play with, you little syllable sponge.'

'Sly-able.'

'Syllable.' Kayla squeezed the child in a spontaneous hug. 'That's a nice safe word, isn't it? Syllable.'

'Sly-able.'

'Close enough.' Kayla chuckled, her heart melting. She *was* clucky but the matching requirements, a man and a marriage, were a long way in her future. Still, she felt as though a tiny door had been cracked open in her entrenched rejection of the idea. Jack and Liz had unwittingly helped her see possibilities.

Tom's image slid into her mind and sent her heart ricocheting around her ribcage.

God, she'd only just allowed herself to think abstractly that strong men weren't all bad news. No way was she ready to start thinking about a specific man.

She had plans. If there was one thing she'd learned from her father it was the value of having plans, setting goals and achieving them.

She'd learned a lot about herself in the weeks she'd been in Dustin. Especially in the last two weeks—and, disturbingly, most of it through her contact with Tom. When she left here, she'd be grateful to him.

As Tom approached the camping area, he spotted Kayla near the door of the van.

Anticipation tightened his muscles. He slowed to a halt, forcing a breath deep into his lungs, willing himself to relax.

Kayla.

His date.

She was a visual feast, long and slender and willowy, with little Emma bouncing on her hip. A fitted pale blue top moulded to her breasts, hugging the narrowness of her waist before flaring over the swell of her hips. Navy slacks clung to the slender curves of her legs and buttocks. Unable to resist, his eyes skimmed down to her gently swaying hips, to Emma's chubby little leg wrapped monkey style around Kayla's waist. She carried the child easily, stronger than her slender frame implied. Her upper body was tilted slightly to one side, a cantilever to accommodate the little girl's weight. The posture was appealingly elegant.

Oh, hell. He blew out a long breath, glad she hadn't spotted him yet. Glad he had a moment to get his reactions under control. He'd promised to be on his best behaviour tonight but it wasn't going to be easy.

He wanted Kayla.

Badly.

She turned to speak to someone in the van and he could see her face was relaxed and happy.

Suddenly, Emma saw him and gurgled with excitement, her little hands waving. Kayla turned and he was surprised to see a quick rush of pink to her cheeks.

Such a contrast to the take-charge medical professional who'd handled Ryan earlier today. This Kayla looked self-conscious. But it was the way the laughter in her face faded that made his mood plummet.

That was the look he wanted to banish. The wariness, that visceral reaction, the instinctive closing down, preparation for something unpleasant.

He could see the moment she pulled herself up, making the effort to relax.

One day soon, he wanted to see a completely different look on her face in greeting. Something welcoming, warmer...*no, damn it*, hotter. He wanted hotter.

'You're here,' she said faintly.

'In the flesh.'

At his words, her gaze dropped to his chest, flicked across his shoulders. She looked uncomfortable. He took a deep breath and her eyes skittered away. A stilted silence descended and he felt as callow as a teenager on his first date. He cleared his throat. 'So, are you ready to go?'

'Oh, I hope you don't mind but I, um, thought it'd be nice to walk over with Liz and Jack.'

'Nice? Or safe?'

'Both perhaps.' She fixed him with a wily look as she tucked a strand of honey-blonde hair behind her ear. 'But, then, I don't need to worry about safety, do I? You promised to be on your best behaviour.'

'So I did.' He swallowed. *And I will be—best behaviour... if it kills me.*

'Good,' she said, her face settling into an expression of serene satisfaction.

Tom wanted to reach out, touch her, rattle her again.

Best behaviour, he thought with a touch of desperation. Was the assignment beyond him after all?

Emma reached up to touch one of Kayla's hooped earrings.

'Emmie, hon. I'm attached to that.' She winced and tilted her head to relieve the pull.

Emma's face suddenly screwed up in distress.

'I think she's caught her finger. Let me help.' Tom stepped nearer and bent to the task of freeing the toddler's fingers. As he worked, the feathery ends of Kayla's blonde hair brushed across his knuckles and her fresh, delicious fragrance filled his head. He had to force himself to concentrate when all he really wanted to do was bury his face in the soft skin at the nape of her neck.

After a moment, Emma was free and she switched her attention to him, patting his face. His fingers fumbled to catch the jewellery as it slipped from Kayla's ear.

'It's come out. The catch must have unhooked,' he said, straightening. 'Do you want me to take Emma while you refasten it?'

'Oh, thanks. That'd be great.' She sounded as breathless as he felt.

He tucked the earring into his shirt pocket and held his hands out to Emma. 'Going to come to me, mischief?'

Emma held her hands out and began jiggling on Kayla's hip. 'Yes. Up.'

Kayla bent close to make the transfer easier. Tom slid his arm around the toddler, conscious of Kayla's warmth. When he brushed her midriff, she gasped. Her wide, startled eyes flew to his. He looked down into the crystalline grey irises as dark awareness flared in her inky pupils. He was dimly aware of Emma's arms latching onto him as he stared helplessly, his breath frozen in his chest. Then Kayla blinked and looked away, releasing him from the spell. Elation and hope swelled in his heart, making him giddy. She *was* just as affected by this charge between them as he was.

On impulse, he leaned down and quickly pressed his mouth to Kayla's soft, warm cheek.

'You look lovely,' he murmured.

Fabulous, delicious...edible. But, then, he knew he'd think she looked pretty good in a chaff sack...even better in nothing at all. An ache of need spread through his gut.

'Thanks,' she said, a tiny rough catch in her voice. 'Could I have m-my earring please?' She held out her hand.

He reached into his pocket for the bauble and deposited it on her palm.

She turned away, tilting her head so she could guide the earring back into place. Her hair swung in a silky curtain to hide her face.

'Kay-lah.' Emma wriggled then looked at him expectantly.

'Yes, that's Kayla.'

'Oh, no.' Kayla twisted back to give the toddler a despairing look. 'No, Emmie, hon, remember your new word for today is syllable.'

With delighted giggles, Emma clapped her hands. 'Kay-lah. Cluck-ee.'

Tom's tension evaporated abruptly. He grinned broadly and looked back at mortified Kayla as fresh colour flooded across her cheeks.

'Kay-lah. Cluck-ee.'

'Is she, now?'

Kayla groaned. 'You know she doesn't have any idea

what she's saying. She's playing with words and sounds. Unfortunately, those two words have taken her fancy.'

'Bad luck,' Tom said gently.

'Yes.'

His heart lurched at the way her mouth pouted slightly. 'It could be worse.'

'I'm trying to imagine,' she drawled, fixing him with a disbelieving look.

'Oh, definitely. Much worse.' He collected his wits. 'It could have been a swear word. When Ry was about Emma's age, he came over to my place with his dad and went home saying *buddy*. Charlotte thought it was cute until she realised he was actually saying...er—' He stopped and glanced at Emma, who was fingering the logo on his T-shirt. He'd better spell the word just to be on the safe side. 'B-L-O-O-D-Y.'

Kayla chuckled and her eyes sparkled. 'Okay, yes. That is bad.'

'Cluck-ee,' Emma chirped looking from one to the other smugly.

'But so is this.' Kayla huffed out a sigh. 'Everyone who hears her is going to think I'm...'

'Wanting to start a family?' He struggled to keep his voice light. The thought of Kayla's belly round with child made his stomach curl with hunger.

'Yes.' Kayla sent him resigned look under her lashes. She looked so adorable, so desirable. The tension in his gut cranked up another notch.

He was starting to fit her into the mould of the woman he wanted to keep. Was it too soon for that? His head was telling him, yes, it was too soon...but his heart was telling him to go for broke.

Kayla walked beside Tom, acutely aware of his every stride.

Emma was balanced easily on his hip. He hadn't relinquished the toddler; instead he'd offered to carry her. Kayla wished she could put his domesticity down to a misguided attempt to impress but she knew it would be unfair. He was too relaxed, Emma was too comfortable, too familiar with him for it to be a rare event.

Tom Jamieson was genuine. Kayla's heart gave a painful squeeze. *Strength and tenderness all wrapped up in a ruggedly attractive package.*

She was charmed and dismayed in equal measure. His treatment of Ryan and Emma pierced her careful safeguards, leaving her feeling unsettled, susceptible. She was really seeing him, being forced to put aside her preconceived ideas about who he was.

How odd that this weekend of competitive rough-and-tumble sport should showcase such extraordinary sensitivity. The sooner it was over the better. Back in the hospital flat, in town and working—that was what she needed so she could get some perspective.

'Cluck-ee.'

Kayla rolled her eyes to find Tom's amused gaze on her.

'She'll find something new soon.'

'Promise?' She managed a smile. 'Though perhaps you're right. I shouldn't complain. The next thing she latches onto might be worse.'

'With a bit of luck, you won't have to worry about her chattering tonight. With all the fresh air and running around today, she must be worn out. She'll be out like a light after tea.'

As though she'd understood his words, Emma yawned hugely and her head drooped onto Tom's shoulder, her thumb in her mouth. Tom tilted his head and laid his cheek on the snuggling toddler's hair. Kayla's heart melted. She tried to imagine her own father carrying Maddy or herself the way Tom held Emma.

The picture wouldn't come. If her father had a softer side, she and Maddy had never seen it.

Tom's short dark hair was damp and sleek, and she realised he must have found time to bathe between helping to set up for the evening and coming to collect her.

No shave, though. Dark stubble shadowed his jaw. It looked good on him. She'd felt it when he'd bent to kiss her on the cheek. Along with a soft warmth and a hint of moisture with the brush of his lips. She raised her fingers to her face, remembering. For the tiniest, maddest moment she'd wanted to turn her head, feel that pressure and heat on her mouth.

With his free hand, Tom reached out to capture hers and she forgot all about Emma's word obsession. Pleasantly rough skin slid over hers until they were palm to palm. It had been years since she'd held hands with anyone and she'd forgotten how much she enjoyed it. The few men she'd dated had considered themselves too sophisticated for the simple public gesture.

In this peaceful bush setting, she felt suddenly overwhelmed by a wave of contrasting stimuli. The size and brawny strength of the man beside her, his undeniable masculinity...and yet his poignant gentleness.

And then there was the example of her friends. Jack, so tall and strong...and yet his tenderness with Liz and Emma.

It wasn't...right. It wasn't...the way things were between men and women, between men and children. Her experiences hadn't prepared her for the possibility of beauty and softness in the interactions of strong males with those physically weaker than themselves.

Tom's hand on hers acted as an anchor while she struggled to deal with her impressions.

'All right?' he murmured, as though he sensed her turmoil. And his acute sensitivity to her in this moment just made it worse.

'Of course.' Her throat was raw, her voice rough. She managed a tight smile.

Just as well Tom had reiterated his promise to be on his best behaviour. It was her own impulses that she was starting to worry about.

CHAPTER EIGHT

KAYLA suppressed a quiver as Tom's breath whispered over the tender skin of her ear. 'Prepare yourself to be welcomed into the Jamieson family fold,' he murmured.

'This is *all* your family?' she said, looking around at the laughing, talking crowd. Several children were happily playing a chasing game in and around the standing adults and a group of men holding cans of beer had gathered to commune around a barbecue.

'Lots of them. Don't ask me where everyone fits. Mum knows. Friends, too. The camp draft Saturday night barbecue is something of a tradition.'

A slender brunette who'd just hugged Liz looked in their direction and a huge grin immediately lit her face.

'Remember, you only have to give name, rank and serial number,' Tom said, his voice filled with laughter as the smiling woman hurried towards them. Liz and Jack trailed behind her.

Kayla speared Tom with a short glance. 'Worried I might say something to embarrass you?'

'Nope.' His fingers squeezed hers as he pitched his voice for her alone. 'Worried someone might say something to scare you back into the shell I've winkled you out of.'

'You make me sound like a hermit crab,' she muttered.

Tom's chuckle rumbled in her ears before he said, 'Hi, Mum.'

'I've been keeping an eye out so I didn't miss you two arriving. You must be Kayla.' The dark-haired woman stepped forward, her arms wide in welcome. For a split second as Kayla felt Tom release her hand, she wanted to cling to him. The next she was scooped into a hug. 'You're even more gorgeous than the photo Liz showed me.'

'Kayla, meet my mother, Rosie. Mum, as you've guessed, this is Kayla.'

'I can't tell you how much I've been looking forward to meeting you, my dear.' Rosie held her at arm's length and sent her son a quick look filled with mischief. 'Even more since my son told me he'd asked you as his date for tonight.'

There was that word again. *Date*. Kayla swallowed and pinned a smile on her face. 'It's lovely to meet you, Mrs Jamieson.'

'Rosie, I insist. We're delighted to have you join us tonight. How are you enjoying your time in Dustin so far?'

'Very much, Rosie. It makes a nice change of pace from the city.'

'We're lucky to have you filling in for Liz's maternity leave and I hear I have you to thank for patching up my grandson this morning.'

'Oh, of course. Ryan.' Kayla nodded. 'How is he?'

'Good as gold. He was right here a moment ago. Oh, there you are,' the older woman said as Ryan materialised at her side.

'Hi, Kayla,' the boy said, looking up at her shyly.

'Hello, Ryan.' She smiled at him. 'You got to the barbecue after all.'

'I had a sleep this afternoon so Mum said it was okay.'

'How is your arm?'

'Good, 'cept I can't ride.'

'So you want to get back on, then?' Kayla couldn't hide

her surprise even though a quick glance at Tom suggested this was to be expected.

'Of course.'

'He's a tough little nut. Aren't you, Ry?' said his grandmother as she ruffled his hair.

'Yeah.' Ryan looked as though he'd been paid the highest compliment.

'Reminds me a lot of someone else while he was growing up.' The look Rosie gave her son was filled with equal parts of affection and exasperation. 'Tom gave me more than his fair share of grey hairs. He still does. They're always your children, Kayla, no matter how big and competent they get.'

Kayla's chest tightened unexpectedly at the words. What would it have been like to grow up with someone so firmly in her corner as Rosie obviously was for her children and grandchildren.

'What about Mum?' Ryan asked.

'Her, too. The stories I could tell you.'

'But you'll resist because we don't want to send Kayla hightailing it back to Melbourne, do we, Mum?' Tom said. 'We need her.'

His tone shivered down Kayla's spine. He almost sounded... possessive. The idea should be utterly repugnant but instead she felt a quick, unwelcome stab of feminine curiosity.

'True.' Rosie laughed undaunted by her son's warning. 'But she might like to know what she's letting herself in for.'

Did Rosie mean in Dustin? With the Jamiesons?

Or with Tom? Her heart squeezed painfully.

She was glad Jack chose that moment to come to collect Emma so that Tom was occupied transferring the sleepy toddler. She needed a moment to take a deep breath, pull herself together without his too-perceptive eyes on her.

'Come and get it!' one of the men near the barbecue called out as he transported a laden platter towards the food table.

'Oh, yes, do. Go,' Rosie said, making ushering movements towards the table. 'Food disappears quickly around here.'

'Come on.' Tom captured her hand and tugged her forward. He handed her a plate and a serviette-wrapped set of utensils.

'Kebabs?' Two appeared on her plate. 'Chops? Rissoles? Salad?'

Tom moved with her around the table, efficiently loading up her plate. He did it so naturally she found herself unable to object. 'Let's grab a seat.'

He steadied her while she stepped over the bench then put his plate on the table to save his spot. 'Can I get you something to drink?'

'A small red wine would be lovely.' She watched him walk away. Being cared for the way Tom was looking after her as his date was a new experience. It was both wonderful and unsettling.

'Be right back.' He left his jacket on the seat.

A moment later, a girl bounced onto Tom's jacket and said, 'Hello. Ry said you're the doctor who fixed his arm?'

'That's right. I'm Kayla.' She turned her attention to the feminine version of Ryan. 'Are you Hannah?'

'Yep.' Hannah grinned showing a neat set of orthodontic braces. 'Ry let me sign the plaster already. I was the first.'

'Lucky you,' Tom said, returning with a couple of glasses. He leaned over Hannah to put them on the table.

'Yep, he's pretty good. For a boy.' Hannah grinned at her uncle then turned her ingenuous blue eyes back in Kayla's direction. 'He said it hurt a lot when he fell off but that he didn't cry.'

'Your brother was very brave,' Kayla said.

'Hannah, come and get your dinner, please,' Charlotte called from the food table. She waved to Kayla and said, 'Hi, Kayla, glad you could join us. Hannah, any time today would be good, please.'

Kayla waved back, watching a reluctant Hannah do her mother's bidding. 'She's going to be a heartbreaker when she gets older.'

'I think Charlie's hoping that contempt for boys stays with her for another ten years.' Tom climbed over the seat. As he settled beside her, his thigh brushed hers, sending a crazy fizz of sensation over her skin. 'You protected Ryan. I half expected you to give Hannah the line about tears being nothing to be ashamed of.'

Kayla cleared her throat. 'For a start, it's not a line. And, secondly, I figure it falls under the heading of patient confidentiality.'

'I'm glad.' He twisted towards her and smiled, his eyes warmly approving. Heat came off his body in waves that enveloped her. She stared at him helplessly as he spoke. 'Han's a sweetheart deep down but she's hiding it under a thick layer of holy terror at the moment.'

Someone called his name and he turned away. Kayla blew out a small breath of relief. Being the focus of Tom's attention was not getting any easier. The man had some serious chemistry.

Other friends and family members joined them at the long table and the conversation became general. His family were fun, lively, affectionate and friendly. As she chatted, Kayla tried to convince herself that she'd imagined her response to Tom. But almost as though he understood what was going on in her mind, Tom turned to touch her. His hand lingered on her shoulder while he asked her to pass the salt, then stroked down to the small of her back as she leaned forward to get it.

'Thanks.' His fingers closed over hers briefly as she tried to place the container on the table in front of him.

Nothing objectionable, just enough to ensure all her senses were tuned to him.

Every time he spoke.

Every time he shifted on the bench seat.

Her very cells seemed to be anticipating the next time he might touch her.

'Kayla?' Her name spoken in a soft girl's voice was accompanied by a light tug on her sleeve. She turned to see Hannah, her elbow on the table and her face propped in her hand.

'Yes, Hannah.'

'Are you in love with Uncle Tom?'

Kayla blinked at the child, feeling a rush of heat running into her cheeks. She sensed Tom's stillness beside her and she didn't dare look in his direction. The gathering twilight would help to hide the betraying colour—she hoped.

'I'm sure he's, um, very loveable, Hannah,' she said, selecting her words carefully. 'And I bet you love him very much.'

'Yes, but he's my uncle so I have to.'

'Right.' Kayla met the still-questioning blue eyes. 'You see, I've only just met him, so it's too soon to know.' She only just stopped the *yet* that was ready to trip off her tongue.

'But you like him, right?' the child persisted, and Kayla had a sudden sympathy for Ryan wanting to keep his tears a secret.

'Yes, I like him. He's a nice man.' She heard Tom's soft chuckle. 'But if he's not careful, that could change.'

'Why would it change?' The girl frowned.

Kayla suppressed a sigh. 'I'm teasing you, Hannah.'

'Oh.' Hannah nodded, her expression plainly saying she'd never understand the vagaries of adult humour. 'Good. You're the first girlfriend that Uncle Tom's had for ages. Nana said ever since—'

'Dessert's up, Han,' Tom said. 'I heard Aunty Doreen was bringing her peppermint and chocolate pavlova,' Tom said. 'You don't want to miss out.'

The child was gone in a flash.

'Great magic trick, *Uncle Tom*.' Kayla slid him a disgusted look. 'Pity you didn't perform it five minutes earlier.'

'But I was learning so much. A man's gotta do what a man's gotta do.' He reached out and his fingers brushed her hair back over her ear in a slow caress that left her breathless.

'Not when he's promised to be on his best behaviour,' she murmured.

'Ah, yes.' His hooded gaze was darker, sharper, holding her captive for a moment before sliding down to her mouth. A sharp stab of longing shocked her. 'You could always release me from my promise.'

Her heart slammed into her ribs as she wrenched her eyes away from him to look around the table. Everyone else was talking as though nothing out of the ordinary had happened. It was only her world that had been shaken.

'I could.' She reached for her glass. The liquid sloshed as she picked it up. 'But I don't think I will.'

'But you want to. Admit it,' he said, his words laced with sinful temptation.

Damn it. He was right.

Her mouth was drier than the dust on the dirt road. God, what had made her think she could indulge in repartee with Tom and get away with it.

'Name, rank and serial number, didn't you say?'

His delicious, low chuckle hummed across her senses.

Tom looked over to where Kayla was helping pack away the last of the dishes. Jack and Liz had returned to camp much earlier with little Emma snuggled up fast asleep in a sleeping bag.

Kayla had insisted on staying to help, mucking in willingly with the clean-up. He wondered if she realised the consequence of that—she'd have to walk back to camp with him.

Alone.

Tom swallowed. Him and Kayla.

Just the two of them.

Best behaviour.

Dating Kayla required strategy. Like camp drafting. Rush in too soon and he risked spooking his elusive quarry. The trick was to balance patience with decisive action at the right time and right place. He was a champion camp draft rider. He only hoped he had the strength and sensitivity to apply patience and pressure at the right times and places with Kayla.

He suppressed a chuckle. Would Kayla appreciate his analogy for their fledgling relationship? He thought she might with her quick, wicked sense of humour. He enjoyed it…he enjoyed her. His gut tightened.

He dropped the tied rubbish bag into the bin and turned back towards the barbecue area in time to see Kayla throw her head back to laugh at something with his mother. She appeared to have enjoyed herself tonight with his family. And that was important to him. He loved his family.

He walked slowly back towards the two women.

He hadn't brought anyone home to meet his family for years. Not since he'd been shot. No wonder Hannah had picked up on the family scuttlebutt. His then girlfriend had dumped him while he still lay in hospital, tubes threading through his body. Marissa hadn't wanted to stay at his bedside to play nursemaid to an invalid. He'd had a lucky escape there, in more ways than one. Her defection hadn't surprised him… and it hadn't hurt him either. Except for his pride.

A band of tension circled his chest. He had the feeling Kayla could hurt him badly.

But he was going to make his move anyway.

Did that make him a fool? He frowned.

'Thanks for your help, Kayla.'

'My pleasure, Rosie. I've had a lovely evening.'

'Ready to go?' His question came out more harshly than he'd meant and both women looked at him in surprise.

'Yes. I'll just get my jumper,' Kayla said.

He consciously eased the muscles across his shoulders. 'I've got it here.'

'Goodnight, Kayla,' his mother said. 'I'll look forward to seeing you again soon.'

'Goodnight, Rosie.'

''Night, Mum.'

He settled his hand in the small of Kayla's back, feeling her body heat through his palm, the rub of her clothing at each step a small torturous friction

Silence closed around them, only broken by the soft rustle of dry leaves beneath their feet. The lamp he held played over the ground around them. Diffused light enclosing them in a golden bubble of intimacy.

'Penny?' he said, reaching out to capture her hand.

She chuckled softly. 'I was just thinking that all this is so different from the things I usually do on a night out.'

'Different good or different bad?'

'Oh, different good, definitely. I really did have a great time. I wasn't just saying that.' Her teeth glinted briefly in the pale oval of her face. 'Your family is wonderful. Special.'

'I think so, too.'

After a moment, he said, 'What sort of things are a usual night out for you?'

'Nothing very dashing. Juggling a social life can be hard when you work odd hours. But I like the occasional movie, maybe a light opera. Maybe a bike ride along the Yarra.'

With her fiancé, probably. Tom clenched his jaw. He didn't ask. He didn't want to know.

Tonight, *he* was the man here with Kayla in the dim light, surrounded by towering gums. It was his fingers curled around the fragile bones of her clever healer's hand. He felt ten feet tall.

'I enjoy meeting friends for dinner,' she said. 'Or having them over to my place.'

'Are you an adventurous cook?'

She laughed and he thought he detected an underlying note of bitterness. 'You must have realised by now, I'm not an adventurous anything.'

'Not true. You've uprooted yourself to come to Dustin. You've attended your first camp draft. You've survived an evening with the Jamiesons.'

'Mmm, when you put it like that, I'm positively intrepid.' Her laughter this time was light and the teasing, joyous note rippled across his senses, making him smile.

'You are,' he murmured.

A low whicker greeted them as they reached the edge of their camp.

'There,' he said. 'Even Ziggy agrees.'

'Straight from the horse's mouth?' She chuckled as her footsteps slowed then stopped at her tent. 'Ziggy recognises your voice.'

'Yeah.' Tom rubbed his thumb over her knuckles. 'And he likes his chances of another biscuit of hay.'

'Are they good? His chances?' Her voice was soft.

'Better than average.' He looked down at their still-clasped hands. 'I'd planned on giving him something else before I turned in.'

'Well, I'd better let you get on with it.' There was the tiniest tremor in her words.

'Kayla?' He stepped closer to her, felt the heat of her body reaching out to his. 'I'm going to step out of line.'

She looked up at him. He felt the small shudder that shook her. 'Are you?'

'Yes.' He ran his finger tips up her arm. 'What are you going to do about it?'

'N-nothing.'

Lifting his free hand slowly, he cupped her face, feeling the soft skin against his palm, the cool silk of her hair across his fingers. She tilted her head, offering her mouth to him.

He could feel the tension in her, watched as her lips parted slightly and she bit down on her bottom lip for a tiny second then released it so it plumped back up.

He leaned forward slowly, gave her time to stop him. Her eyelids drifted shut. Over the thunder of his heart, he heard her quick, shuddering breath.

And then his lips touched hers, pressing gently, and everything else became irrelevant. The sensation was electric, exquisite. He rubbed his mouth across hers slowly, backwards and forwards. The sweet softness gave under the pressure, inviting, making him want more than he should on a first kiss.

Eyes shut, he savoured the explosion of taste. Delicious. Exciting. He was drowning, drenched in need.

Her fingers wrapped around his wrist. Flexing once, twice, as though she was debating whether to tug his hand away. But in the end she just held him as though anchoring herself.

He drew her bottom lip into his mouth with gentle suction and ran his tongue over the succulent flesh. Then reluctantly let it go.

Pulling back slowly, he struggled to surface. Kayla didn't move for a long moment, her mouth still offered up to his, swollen, inviting. Unbearably tempting.

Her eyes opened. He heard the shaky breath she sucked in, saw her breasts rise and fall. He clenched his jaw with the effort of not plunging back to take more. He wanted to drop the lamp he held, bury his fingers deep in her hair, use both hands so he could tip her head and take their kiss to a whole new level. Pull her under into the tide of excitement that was raging through him, threatening to sweep him away.

But he had to resist. He wasn't in this for a quick tumble. He wanted more, wanted it all. This was for keeps. The thought crystallised. She was what he wanted for his future.

Reining back his lust, he pressed a kiss to each corner of her mouth and stepped back.

'Let's get you into your tent.' His voice was hoarse.

'M-my tent?' She sounded as dazed as he felt.

'Yeah. While I still remember my promise to behave,' he muttered as he bent to unzip the door. His fingers fumbled with the tab but after a moment he had it open so he could usher her in. 'There you go.'

'Th-thanks.' She bent and stepped into the tent. 'Goodnight, Tom.'

With a sense of desperation, he quickly zipped the door closed before he could disgrace himself by begging. With his fingertips touching the nylon lightly, he closed his eyes and swallowed hard. His mouth still throbbed from her kiss. 'Goodnight, Kayla. Sleep well.'

Not waiting for a reply, he turned to walk towards the float and Ziggy's hay supply.

Kayla had kissed him. Progress. Elation and frustration coursed through him. He'd achieved more than he'd expected, less than he'd wanted.

Ziggy whickered again as Tom snipped the hay band. He tossed a biscuit of hay into the corral.

With one last look towards Kayla's tent, he unzipped his own nylon igloo and crawled inside.

He stripped and climbed into his swag. Eyes open, he rolled over, looking in the direction of Kayla's tent. Was she snuggled into her sleeping bag now? Unable to resist torturing himself a little, he tried to picture her. Pyjamas? Naked? He swallowed as a cold sweat broke across his skin.

Bad idea.

He turned to lie on his back. He wanted to get her into bed, desperately. But more than that, he wanted to look after her, cherish her, erase the sadness he sensed in her. She presented a tough, capable exterior—and she was all those things. But underneath there was a sweet, vulnerable woman.

A city girl who fitted in with his town, his family. And, most of all, with him.

CHAPTER NINE

KAYLA woke the next morning to the snap of twigs and the smell of wood smoke. When she opened her eyes and saw the faint glow of light through dark blue nylon, it took her a moment to remember where she was.

She lay for a moment, listening to masculine voices talking softly. A low masculine chuckle sent a shiver down her spine.

Tom.

He'd kissed her...she'd let him. More than that, she'd *wanted* him to. Her heart lurched as she lifted her fingers to touch her lips. His mouth on hers had been quite simply mind-blowing.

For all her fine thoughts that she couldn't get involved, it had been Tom who'd called a halt last night.

Footsteps moved away and the voices faded then stopped altogether.

Hiding out in the tent was appealing but not realistic—she needed to face Tom some time today. Training of a lifetime said it might as well be sooner rather than later. Cool air hit her skin as she wriggled out of the sleeping bag. She grabbed her clothes and pulled them on, then ran a brush through her hair. When she got home tonight, she'd enjoy a nice hot shower. Perhaps that was one of the attractions of camping—returning to the benefits of civilisation gave them a disproportionate decadence.

She unzipped the tent and clambered out into a pale misty morning. Light slanted in ethereal golden beams, catching on the smoky fogginess and silhouetting the trees. Sounds of campers stirring at the sites around them was dampened by the mist. The musical chink of metal hitting metal, a hushed voice, horses neighing.

A small distance away from her tent, a fire crackled. A billy was just starting to steam and a big black cast-iron pot sat in coals at the edge.

The scene delighted her with its natural innocence. She stretched and grinned, feeling an unfamiliar sense of peace settle over her. The air she inhaled smelled of smoke and earth and eucalyptus and…horse. She liked the basic rawness of it.

Who'd have thought there was a corner of her that would enjoy camping? Not that she'd had to do anything useful herself, she thought, huffing out a small laugh. Jack had set her tent up and Tom's family had fed her last night so she could hardly congratulate herself on being intrepid and resourceful. Still, she was…having fun. Frivolous, naive, unsophisticated fun.

Tom came back into view from behind the horse float and the lovely calmness evaporated abruptly. She felt her smile falter as he walked towards her.

'Good morning, Kayla.' He lingered over her name as though savouring a particularly interesting flavour. She suppressed a quiver. Warm intimacy glowed in his eyes as though they shared something special.

Which they had…

Her eyes moved to his mouth and she had to consciously stop herself from moistening her lips.

'Good morning.' The sound was little more than a croak. She cleared her throat.

'I've got coffee on,' he said. 'Can I tempt you?'

'Yes, please.' She winced. With the direction of her thoughts, *tempt* seemed to be the perfect word for everything about Tom Jamieson.

He moved over to the fire and hunkered down to lift off the pot. There was something very potent about the way his moleskins pulled taut over his buttocks and clung to lean, straight thighs. From the chunky navy jumper that moulded to his broad shoulders to the well-worn leather boots on his feet, he exuded a vital masculinity. She'd never have predicted that she could be susceptible to the cowboy image. But she was. Oh, God! Was she ever!

He straightened and handed her a mug.

'Thanks.' She took the drink, wrapping her fingers around the warm china and trying to collect her scattered wits.

'Sleep well?'

The simple question reminded her of the long minutes that she'd lain awake, straining her ears for every little sound he'd made. Torturing herself with her imagination, wondering what every little rustle might be. She felt her cheeks warm.

'Very,' she croaked, then cleared her throat. 'All that fresh air knocks us city slickers around.'

He tilted his head and slid her a teasing look. 'Need some exhaust fumes to re-tox you?'

'That's right.' She chuckled, feeling her tension subsiding.

He bent back over the fire and tapped the cast-iron pot with his fingertips. 'How does breakfast of damper with baked beans, eggs and bacon sound?'

'Wicked. Irresistible.' Saliva filled her mouth. 'About a million miles away from the healthy balanced meal I usually call breakfast but I'm game.'

Her reward was a big smile.

She swallowed. 'Do you want a hand?'

'Have you cooked over a campfire before?'

'First-timer camper, I'm afraid. Never a Girl Guide.'

'In that case, grab a seat and supervise this time.' He picked up a pair of leather gloves and a small shovel and began spreading glowing coals out from the fire. 'Next time, maybe we'll get you more hands on.'

Next time. There wouldn't be a next time, but it seemed churlish to point that out. Even more confusing was the way her heart squeezed with a pang of strong regret that there *wouldn't* be another opportunity.

She shook off the feeling. Sure, the camping weekend was turning into an unexpected treat—but part of that was probably the novelty of it. And the novelty of Tom—he'd challenged her out of her usual reservations and she was still struggling to find her equilibrium.

Liz joined her. While Jack arranged the chairs so his pregnant wife was sitting with her feet up, Emma crawled onto Kayla's knee.

'This is the life, don't you think?' Liz gave her an impish grin as Jack turned to join Tom at the fire.

'Sitting around a campfire?' Holding her hot drink out to the side so Emma couldn't spill it, Kayla brushed her hand over Emma's curls.

'Yes, there's something about roughing it that makes the man in your life take over domestic chores and demonstrate his survival skills.'

Kayla was helpless to stop her gaze from straying to Tom. He was breaking eggs, one-handed, into a bowl suggesting he was no stranger to cooking.

The man in your life. Not that he was the man in her life… She didn't want a man in her life right now but if she did…

'And the view's not half bad, is it?' Liz murmured.

Heat scorched across Kayla's cheeks, momentarily frying her thought processes as surely as the bacon that was sputtering in the pan. She couldn't meet Liz's eyes. 'They work well together, don't they? Jack and Tom. Do the three of you do this often? Camping, I mean?' Smooth change of subject. Yep, no way was Liz going to notice that. Kayla stifled a sigh. Dustin's police sergeant was turning her into a jabbering wreck, hardly able to string a sensible sentence together, and she didn't have the faintest idea of how to regain her customary poise.

Tom moved over to the other side of the fire and crouched at the pot with the beans. The murmur of Kayla and Liz talking in the chairs nearby was nearly drowned by the sizzling bacon. He stirred the bubbling beans and flicked a glance towards the women. Emma had settled on to Kayla's lap, looking right at home. Warm longing wrapped around his heart, making it hard to breathe.

He realised Liz was watching him with a thoughtful look. Would she feel obliged to give him another warning about Kayla? He didn't feel as though he deserved one but there was no doubting her protective instincts. His intentions were honourable, though given half a chance he sure would like to take some dishonourable shortcuts.

He looked down into the beans.

'The damper's ready and so's the bacon,' Jack said, interrupting his reverie.

Tom nodded and checked the temperature of the second pan. 'Eggs coming right up.'

Time to get his mind back on the meal. He had some ideas for social gatherings this week, nothing too obvious that Kayla would baulk at. A little patience here, a little pressure there. Already she was starting to look at him with less instinctive wariness after their talk yesterday. Great strategy as long as he could keep himself reined in.

Kayla enjoyed the second day at the arena, glad her professional services weren't required. A couple of minor falls resulted in nothing more than injured pride for the competitors involved. Before the afternoon was over she'd been invited to the post-camp draft celebration at the pub, a darts tournament to watch Tom's father play on Wednesday, his mother's birthday on Thursday and to Tom's traditional Friday night marinara get-together.

Her social calendar looked suddenly exciting…and full of opportunities to see Tom.

Friday evening arrived and Kayla followed Tom's directions. Past a white weatherboard house, a small dip with a grove of gums and then, on the left, brick pillars and wrought-iron gates.

She turned in and accelerated cautiously down the long driveway. Horses grazed in the paddocks to either side, including Ziggy from the camp draft in the paddock nearest the house.

Her car was the only one in the gravel circle in front of the big, old house. Her stomach swooped and she took a deep breath into her diaphragm to relax the tension. The others would arrive soon, so she wouldn't be alone with Tom for long.

Gathering up her bag and the bottle of wine she'd bought, she slipped out of the car and looked at the house. Wonderful wide verandas encased the three sides and two large chimneys in the roof hinted at cosy fire-heated rooms on wintry nights. There were signs of work in progress on the primer-coated window-sills and a couple of sawhorses at one corner of the veranda.

The door was open but she rang the doorbell anyway.

'Come on through,' Tom called from somewhere deep in the house. 'Straight down the hall, the kitchen's on the left. You can't miss me.'

'Okay.' She walked along the hall, glancing in the rooms off to each side. Comfortable furniture in the lounge, a big king-sized bed in another room.

He stood at the stove. With his back to her, she took the

opportunity to look her fill for a few precious seconds. Short dark hair, broad shoulders hugged by a white T-shirt, his long, lean body. Whipcord muscles in his arms working as he lifted the pot. A tea-towel wrapped around his waist and tucked into the waistband of his low-slung jeans.

Her gaze tracked down until she reached his bare feet on the black and white tiles.

'Hi. I was starting to think you'd got lost.'

She dragged her eyes up to meet his. 'Hi. I was just...' *Ogling you.* No, that would never do. She searched for a different topic. A rich tomato aroma wafted to her. 'Something smells wonderful.'

He gave her a wide smile. 'Mmm, I hope it's dinner.' He picked up a spoon from the bench and dipped it into the pot then turned and walked towards her. 'Taste.'

The sauce-covered spoon hovered at her mouth with his hand cupped underneath to catch drips. He looked at her expectantly and after a tiny hesitation she leaned forward to sample. The flavour was every bit as full bodied and fabulous as it smelled. 'Delicious.'

He leaned down to kiss her, his tongue stroking delicately along her bottom lip. His cheeks creased with a smile when he pulled back. 'Mmm, not bad at all.'

Her pulse raced at the heat in his eyes.

'You don't think it needs more salt?' he said, and she struggled to make sense of his words. 'The sauce?'

She shook her head, unable to speak.

'Okay, good.'

When he turned away and walked back to the stove, she managed to drag a deep breath into her lungs, feeling almost light-headed with relief.

'Make yourself at home.'

'Thanks,' she said, glad her voice didn't betray any of the internal shaking she was feeling. She glanced around the room, taking in the modern adaptation of an old-style kitchen. Weathered Baltic pine cupboards and hutches, wide polished benches. An old, ornate cast-iron wood stove in the wall, copper hooks with pans and other utensils hanging from a rack over the bench. 'I brought a white wine since you said it was marinara.'

'Thanks.' He took the bottle and put it in the fridge to keep chilled.

'Can I help?'

'Sure. Do you want to set the table? I've got everything laid out.' He waved at the neat stack of cutlery and crockery on the island bench. 'I just hadn't had a chance to finish.'

Then she noticed that there was two of everything—plates, glasses, cutlery. 'I thought you were having lots of people over for dinner.'

'Not tonight. There's salad already made up in the fridge and dressing too.'

'So it's just the two of us?'

'Yes.' He slanted a surprised look at her as he picked up a dish mounded with thick golden straps of uncooked pasta. 'Is that a problem?'

'Yes. No. Maybe.' Tension tightened her jaw as she looked at him. 'You said it was a tradition for you to have friends over for marinara on Friday nights.'

'It is. This week, I'm having one special friend over. You.' He turned away to the pots and said casually, 'Once I put the pasta and the marinara on to cook it won't take long.'

Kayla chewed her lip for a moment then shrugged and picked up the plates. It was obviously her misunderstanding and she wasn't going to turn around and go home now. He hadn't put a foot wrong and she didn't feel unsafe with him. She did feel unsettled, on edge, but not in any way threatened.

At the table, she saw he'd put out two plain utilitarian white candles. The makeshift holders, empty fruit juice bottles, were a sweet touch and somehow more seductive than if he'd been able to produce formal candlesticks.

Tom brought over an ice bucket with the now opened bottle of wine. He poured wine into the glasses then handed her one and chinked the lip of his against hers. 'Cheers.'

'Cheers.'

'Nice. Good choice,' he said after a quick sip. 'Everything's ready. I just need to drain the pasta and bring it over. Sit.'

She watched him move around the kitchen. Confident and graceful, a man at home in his skin. He made a very appealing picture...far too appealing.

She lowered her gaze to the table. 'You've left the matches here—shall I light the candles?'

'Yes, please.' He lifted the mounded bowls and walked towards her.

'That looks like real home-made pasta,' she said as he put them on the table.

'It is.' He used a pasta ladle to pick up a scoop of spaghetti and transferred it to her plate. From the other bowl he lifted a generous serving of the sauce. 'Only the best for my marinara.'

'Who made it for you?'

'Made it myself.' There was a small secret smile playing around his mouth.

'You *made* the pasta? *Real* pasta?'

'Yep.'

She gave an uncertain laugh. 'Right. Jamieson is obviously a good, solid Italian name.'

He raised his brows and gave her an affronted look, which was spoiled by the way his dark brown eyes sparkled with mischief. 'I'll have you know that my grandmother is Italian. I learned to make pasta from an expert.'

'Okay, okay.' She held her hands up in a mock surrender. 'I apologise. You've done an amazing job.'

'Thank you.' He rewarded her with a big smile. After filling a bowl for himself, he slipped into the seat across the table from her. 'Dig in.'

She twirled the pasta onto her fork and lifted it. The strands melted in her mouth. 'Oh. My. Goodness.' She took a second mouthful. 'Mmm, I think I've died and gone to heaven. This is seriously delicious.'

He grinned. 'Glad you like it.'

'Like it? I love it.' She took another mouthful. 'You are deservedly famous for your spaghetti marinara.'

Tom watched her eating the food he'd prepared. Her genuine relish gave him a good feeling. Even though he knew it had been hard for her once she'd realised she was his only guest for dinner, she'd still decided to trust him enough to relax anyway. That was a huge step and he had to be careful not to abuse that. He could tuck his needs ruthlessly back into line. Tonight was about laying more groundwork. Just as well he was a patient man.

'Tell me about growing up with a deputy commissioner for a father,' he said.

'Wow.' She stopped and blinked at him. 'There's a leap into a tough topic.'

'I want to know about you. How else will I learn if I don't ask the hard questions?' He grinned at her. 'I should also point out that you've avoided the question so that tells me a whole lot, too.'

'Now you're scaring me.'

He picked up his wine and took a sip, letting the silence grow.

She shrugged and looked down at her plate. 'Dad was working towards his promotion when I was growing up. Of course...like anything, it had good points and bad points. He tried to run the household like a mini police academy. Not altogether a success.' She gave him a small smile. 'On the other hand, by the time I left high school I was good at self-discipline, delayed gratification, problem-solving and goal-setting.'

She huffed out a small self-mocking laugh. 'And my boy-friends were *very* well behaved. I was always home before curfew, no octopus hands, no love bites, no whisker burn, no rumpled clothing.' Using her fork, she twirled spaghetti onto the tines and took a mouthful.

'Does that count as a good point or a bad one?'

She finished chewing and swallowed. 'Excellent question. I'm not sure. I think maybe it stunted the development of my feminine wiles.'

'Believe me, honey,' he murmured, as he speared a prawn then looked at her, 'those have developed just fine.'

She regarded him for a moment then with the tiniest move-ment of her shoulder she said, 'Maybe.' Her gaze dropped to her plate.

It was obvious she didn't believe him. Kayla was beautiful, courageous and competent. Confident, too—except for a large blind spot about her own value. Surely, a father's job was to give his children belief in themselves and their abilities?

The way his own father had done for him.

The way he wanted to do for his children.

Tom swallowed his mouthful of food and turned the con-versation to more general topics. He sensed Kayla's relief and he was rewarded when she relaxed again and opened up more. Her warm laughter rolled over him. He set himself to tease yet another delightful peal out of her.

As he looked his fill, he reflected that he could easily get used to her sitting on the other side of his table...sleeping on the other side of his bed.

At the end of the evening, he followed her home. He waited at the front door while she unlocked it. When she turned back to face him, he moved forward, placed both hands on the brick wall behind her, one each side of her head. She turned her face up for his kiss. His lips sank onto hers, feeling her open to him as he enjoyed her softness, her taste. More. He needed more. His libido strained at the curb bit.

He pulled back and swallowed hard. 'If you're smart, you won't ask me in.'

'Why not?' Her voice was low and husky, delicious.

'I'm in danger of growing tentacles.'

'Tentacles?'

'Like an octopus. Hands everywhere.'

'Oh.' She gave a small nervous laugh. 'Excellent advice, then.'

'Yeah, it is. Go inside and lock the door.' *Quickly.*

As though she'd felt his urgency, she ducked under his arm and slipped through the door. 'Goodnight, Tom.'

Only when he heard the latch snick did he straighten and walk slowly off the porch. With all the self-control he'd been exercising lately, he was going to be eligible for sainthood. But it was worth it.

Kayla listened to Tom's footsteps. Sly images had formed in her mind at Tom's words. How would it be to have his hands on her...everywhere? They were playing with fire and they had to stop. She was glad they'd agreed to be friends—but anything more was impossible. She had to tell him, had to explain why nothing could happen between them.

CHAPTER TEN

LATE afternoon the next day, Kayla stopped at the super-market's refrigerated shelves and studied the selection. The succulent prawns reminded her of Tom's traditional marinara dinner last night. She smiled wryly. She'd half expected him to make a move while he'd had her in the privacy of his home. She'd been prepared, all her defences at the ready, but he'd disarmed her with the care he'd take over dinner. Even with her vulnerability he hadn't stepped out of line.

He'd followed her home and left her on her doorstep after an earth-shattering kiss that had left her close to whimpering. Why hadn't he pressed his advantage? She frowned as another thought occurred to her.

Damn it...she was being manoeuvred as surely as one of his camp draft steers. A little pressure here then none at all when she'd been expecting some. All the while, she'd enjoyed herself, basked in the Jamiesons' readiness to accept her, lapped up Tom's easy companionship because he didn't ask more than she was prepared to give. The camp draft and dinner at the pub to celebrate afterwards, his father's darts tournament, his mother's birthday, the traditional marinara dinner last night.

He was clever. She couldn't help but admire his seduction by stealth. She'd enjoyed every step of the process but it had to stop. They couldn't, mustn't, get any more involved. She had plans.

'I'd prefer a nice juicy steak myself.'

She jolted as a deep masculine voice rumbled in her ear. The plastic-wrapped chicken flew out of her hands. Tom leaned around her, his hand on her shoulder and caught the packet easily on its trajectory back to the supermarket's refrigerated shelf.

'Hello, Kayla.'

'Hi, Tom.' Her mouth split in a wide involuntary smile that refused to be dampened.

He looked pleased as he leaned down to press a quick kiss to her mouth. Her heart stuttered to a stop then raced into a madly erratic gallop.

'Could I have my shopping back, please?' She was proud of how calm she sounded given the hectic things her pulse was doing.

He handed the packet to her. 'You'll need a bit more than that if you're inviting me for dinner at your place.'

'Really?' She rolled her eyes at him and pushed the trolley along to the dairy section. 'Now I see the catch with letting you cook dinner for me last night. You expect me to reciprocate.'

'Caught me out.' He grinned.

She grabbed a tub of plain yoghurt. 'Well, I will—'

'I'm free tonight.' The eagerness on his face was hard to resist.

'I will have you around for dinner,' she said as though he hadn't interrupted, 'with the other people I owe invitations to.'

'You could start with just me tonight.'

'I could. But I don't think I will.'

'Notice too short? You're doing something else?'

'Nope.' She stared sightlessly at the shelves as they meandered past them. At this rate, she was going to get home with none of the things on her list. 'I don't think intimate dinners for two are a good idea.'

'Why not?' He put his hand over hers on the trolley handle.

She stopped and looked at him. 'Because it's asking for trouble.'

'What do you mean?' He tipped his head to one side, his brown eyes intent.

'I'm sure you don't need me to spell that out.'

'You know I can behave myself. Haven't I been good?' His gaze slipped down to her mouth and she knew he was thinking about the kisses they'd shared at the end of each evening.

She looked at the food in her trolley. With the heat radiating from her cheeks, it was a wonder the chicken wasn't grilling right in front of her.

'Mostly,' he said softly.

She refused to think about the *mostly*. He *had* been the perfect gentleman all week. But that didn't make him any less threatening to her. His kisses had been restrained but they still made her feel more than she'd ever felt before. He pushed at her boundaries just by being near her. If he asked for more, she wondered if she'd have the strength to keep saying no. 'You were.'

But she couldn't keep playing with fire or she'd end up roasted. She was moving on in a few months—she needed to keep her eyes on her long-term plans.

'Then how about a meal at the bistro? Plenty of people around. I want to talk to you.'

She tightened her hands around the handle of the trolley. He was right—they did need to talk. There were things she needed to say, too, things to clarify. Meeting on neutral ground at a restaurant would be the best place to do that. Less complicated.

'Kayla?'

She realised her eyes were focussed on Tom's lips. Wrenching her gaze back to his, she said, 'All right.'

He blinked. 'You will?'

'You asked me, didn't you?' she said dryly, oddly satisfied by his scramble to keep up with her abrupt change of mind.

'Yeah, I did, but you looked so intense there for a moment I didn't expect you to agree.' He grinned.

Kayla had to quell a little bubble of treacherous pleasure. He was so sure of himself, it was nice to see him thrown, just a little. 'Yes, well, you're right...we do have things to discuss.'

'Uh-oh. I'm not so sure I like the sound of that.' He looked at her quizzically. 'Should I be worried?'

'Probably.' She couldn't suppress a small smile.

'Oh, Tom, Dr Morgan.' Kayla turned to see a pleasant-faced, plump woman beaming at them. 'I'm so glad to catch the two of you like this. I wanted to thank you. You and Tom saved my Andy's life a couple of weeks ago. At the accident on the main road.'

'Mrs Smyth?' Kayla said.

'Mary, please.'

'Mary. I saw Andy had been transferred home the other day.' She mentally reviewed the patient notes, recalling a stent had been successfully fitted in one of his coronary arteries. 'How is he?'

'He's so much better. We've got an appointment to come and see you next week so you'll see for yourself then. It sounds crazy, and you'd never wish it on anyone, but that accident and his heart attack might be the best things to have happened to our marriage. A real wake-up call for him, for both of us.'

'That's wonderful.' Kayla smiled warmly. 'I'll look forward to seeing the two of you.'

'Anyway, I'm sorry to interrupt. But spotting you together was such a good opportunity to say thank you.' She smiled knowingly, her gaze ping-ponging between her and Tom. 'Anyway, you two have a nice evening.'

Kayla gritted her teeth.

'Thanks, Mary. We will,' Tom said.

'Be careful or you'll really have the grapevine thinking there's something going on,' Kayla said, when the woman had moved on.

'There is.'

'Yes, but…' She huffed out a breath. 'Never mind. What time shall I meet you?'

'I'll pick you up.'

'No,' she said firmly, wanting to circumvent any problems later. 'I might get called out or you might, so I'd prefer to have my car.'

For a moment she thought he was going to argue, but then he nodded. 'Seven o'clock?'

'Okay.'

'You've still got my phone number?'

'Yes.' She gave him a carefully bland look. 'Let me finish my shopping. I'll see you in an hour and a half.'

'See you then.' She watched him walk away, her eyes straying over the broad shoulders and straight back. He moved with a powerful masculine grace, sexy in ways she didn't have any defences against. She reminded herself of all the reasons why getting involved with Tom was a bad idea. Coming to Dustin was just *one* step that she intended to take away from her old life—not the *only* step. Getting involved with anyone was not in her plans—no matter how tempting that *anyone* was.

Tom was such a powerful, compelling man that a woman could get lost in his shadow. Something she didn't want for herself. She'd only just extracted herself from her family's influence, especially from her father's dominance.

Tom turned at the end of the aisle and looked back at her. A jolt like electricity ran through her from head to toe. How much better for her self-respect if she'd moved off as soon as he'd walked away. Instead, he'd caught her loitering beside the breakfast cereals, staring after him like a little lost soul. It was her own fault if he thought she was interested.

He raised his hand in a salute. Sighing, she lifted hers in reluctant acknowledgement.

Oh, yes, he tied her up in nice little knots.

Blast him.

Where was she?

He should have insisted on picking her up. But she'd wanted her car. Miss Independence. Not that he wanted a clinging vine but he hoped it wouldn't be too long before she'd at least accept some things from him.

Tom looked at his watch again and blew out a breath. *Okay, so it wasn't quite seven yet.* God, he'd never been this keyed up about a date in his entire life. To make matters worse, in Kayla's eyes this wasn't even a date—just an opportunity to talk.

He looked around at the door and there she was, speaking to the waitress.

Kayla. One kind of tension eased, only to be replaced immediately by another.

Her fitted dark green top moulded to her breasts, hugging the narrowness of her waist before flaring over the swell of her hips. A multicoloured swirling skirt draped to mid-calf.

He'd always thought short skirts were sexy but Kayla's modest outfit stirred his senses more than any expanse of bare flesh would have. For the first time, he understood why the Victorians considered exposed ankles to be provocative.

His pulse bounded as he imagined his fingers closing like a bracelet around the narrow part of her shin then running up the soft skin. Under the hem of her skirt, over the roundness of her calf, the smoothness of her thighs…

Oh, hell. He blew out a long breath, glad she hadn't spotted him yet. Glad he had a moment to collect himself.

He wanted her.

Badly.

This week of caution and restraint had him champing at the bit. But it was worth it. Kayla was relaxing around him, laughing with him, teasing him. When he'd caught her in the supermarket earlier, her immediate reaction had been a spontaneous smile that had warmed his heart.

The tension between them now was all simmering attraction. He was positive. He was enjoying this slow seduction, enjoying her, the company. Even enjoying the frustration of not getting his own way, having to pursue her, work for her. Taking his time was worth the prize.

She turned and walked in his direction. When she got closer, he rose and held out the chair adjacent to him.

'Thanks.' She smiled at him and slipped into the seat.

The next few minutes were taken up with placing their order.

'What did you want to talk to me about?' Kayla said, her beautiful voice slightly husky.

'Nothing serious until after we've eaten. Better for the digestion.'

'All right. We'll talk about other things.' She straightened her cutlery in a small nervous movement that he found endearing. 'Have you always wanted to be in the police force? Is this what the ten-year-old Tom Jamieson saw himself doing?'

He chuckled. 'My ten-year-old self was a thorough ratbag and if he'd thought about it, he'd probably have seen himself on the other end of the long arm of the law.'

'Really? What saved you from yourself?'

'My parents and the senior constable who worked here at the time conspired to scare me straight.'

'What did you do?'

'Nothing good.'

The silence stretched and her eyebrows rose.

'You know I'm going to annoy you until you tell me,' she said.

'Yeah, I kind of got that feeling. You might not respect me in the morning.'

'Try me.'

A dozen suggestive responses danced on his tongue but he suppressed them all, took a sip of his drink and settled for the truth. 'My cousin and I broke into an uncle's place and liberated some alcohol and cigarettes. Rather a lot of alcohol and cigarettes.'

'Ah.'

He grimaced. 'We made ourselves very, *very* sick.'

'Nasty,' she murmured.

'It was. Our parents made us work on our uncle's place gratis for the Christmas school holidays. Rory and I have both been model citizens ever since.'

'I'm sure.' Her eyes twinkled at him.

The discussion moved on to his work and carried them through the meal. Tom enjoyed telling her about his work, relished the perceptive questions she asked and her insights into human behaviour. In no time at all, the waitress had come back to clear their plates.

In the small silence that followed, he watched Kayla's long fingers stroke the side of her glass.

'Go out with me,' he said, completely forgetting the speech he'd prepared to put his case.

Her eyes lifted to his and he read the conflict there. 'No.'

'Kayla...this chemistry between us isn't something that comes along every day. Aren't you curious about where it might lead?'

'No.' Her response was quick and short. Was she trying to convince him...or herself?

'Are you denying the attraction is mutual?' Let her try, he

thought, remembering their kiss, the response he'd felt in her mobile lips.

'I'm not denying it…but I—I don't want to take it any further.'

Frustration welled up and so did poorly chosen words before he could stop them. 'I'm asking you out on a date, not to leap into bed.'

Her mouth dropped open in a perfect oval of surprise. He shut his eyes and dragged a hand down his face.

'Thank you for clarifying that.' Her voice sounded strangled.

'Bloody hell…why don't I cut my tongue out now?' He could feel the heat crawling into his cheeks. 'All right. I admit it. That thought has crossed my mind, too. What can I say?' He forced his mouth into a wry grin, hoping it might disarm her. 'I'm a man.'

Her eyes were coolly amused. 'Your honesty is…refreshing.'

'Refreshing?' He leaned his elbows on the table and looked at her. 'Is that code for I've completely blown my chances?'

'No, not at all.' She reached for her glass and circled the base on the coaster.

'That's a relief.'

'Your chances were blown before you started.'

'Okay, excellent.' He rubbed his jaw. 'So they haven't got any worse, then.'

There was a small stunned silence and then she laughed. A good sign, considering how far down his throat he'd jammed his foot. He grinned.

After a moment, she sobered. 'I'll level with you, Tom. I can't see the point of getting involved with anyone in Dustin.'

'When you put it like that, a lot of things are pointless, aren't they?' He gave her a long look. 'You might only be here for a short time but that's no excuse not to get involved. With the community, with people.' He reached across the table and laid his fingers over hers. 'With me.'

Her throat moved in a swallow and she watched him steadily. He could see the denial in the pewter depths of her eyes. Desperation spurred him on.

'You're already involved. Look at Mary and Andy. You've profoundly affected their lives. You're friends with Jack and Liz. My mum and dad love you—my whole family loves you. Wherever you go, whatever you do, you'll be involved, whether you like it or not.'

'Yes, I agree as far as the job goes, but it's still temporary. I'm leaving Dustin once Liz's maternity leave is up. I'm only here for the six months. Eight months tops.'

'If you're worried because it's a short stint, we'd find a way to work out the logistics when you go back to Melbourne.' He wasn't ordinarily a fan of long-distance relationships but there were ways around it. Melbourne was only a couple of hours away.

'I'm not going back to Melbourne.'

'Then there's no problem,' he said quickly. 'Stay here.'

She shook her head. 'I'm moving on, Tom. Going north.' Her smile felt like more of a grimace, stiff and unnatural. His enthusiasm and the sincerity behind it had caught her unawares. 'I need to sort myself out, find out what I really want. I've always been good old reliable Kayla. Study hard, don't rock the boat, fill in, help out, don't let anyone down, don't have any inconvenient emotions. I'm rebelling. It's only a decade and a half overdue. No more doormat for me.'

'I don't want to wipe my feet on you, Kayla. How you are in a relationship is a choice. Your choice. If I behave like an idiot, you tell me. You don't let me get away with anything now while we're friends. That won't change if we go out.'

His words held an appealing logic. She had to steel herself against the seductiveness of it.

He leaned forward and reached across the table to take her hands. 'Make me part of your rebellion.'

'What?' She stared at him. 'No.'

'Why not?' His face was alight with enthusiasm.

'Several reasons. Dustin is a small town and you are an important public figure.' She looked at his hand, at the thumb stroking over her knuckles in a long, lazy stroke. 'You can't just run around having affairs.'

'I'm entitled to a private life.'

'But that's it,' she said. 'In Dustin, it wouldn't *be* private.'

'It's still my concern. Tell me what else I'm fighting against here.'

She frowned. 'I'd be using you.'

'It wouldn't be using me if I know and I'm willing.'

'But what if you get hurt.'

'I won't break.' A muscle rippled in his jaw. 'Maybe I'm prepared to take my chances.'

'Maybe I'm not prepared to let you.' She swallowed and lifted her eyes to his. 'Besides, you might hurt me and I'm not prepared to risk that either.'

'Ah.' Humour twinkled in the deep brown eyes that watched her steadily. 'So rebelling safely, then.'

She laughed but even she recognised there was no humour in the sound. 'I guess you caught me out. I can't change everything at once.'

'You're set on this, aren't you?' In the other room, a band struck up couple of notes. Before she could answer, he stood, recapturing her hand. 'Enough talking. Come and dance with me.'

The fast, catchy beat thrummed through her as they entered the larger room. Rock and roll. She loved it.

Tom spun her, controlling her as though she were a top. She laughed with delight and gave herself to the moment, trusting him to catch her. And he did, always, effortlessly.

One song, two. Breathless and energised, she lost count. He

led, she followed. It made her feel alive, hedonistic. Utterly feminine.

Good dancers make good lovers.

Her feet nearly stumbled as her outrageous dance teacher's words slipped into her mind. Tom covered her gaffe, easily pulling her into his flank for another embrace. The move had never seemed so laden with sensuality. She'd done it dozens of times, hundreds of times…but she'd never been so conscious of her body, of her partner's body. The physicality, the sensuality of the dance.

Pressed hip to hip, thigh to thigh. His arm around her, strong and firm. His dark eyes burned down into hers, suddenly predatory as though he could see the question in flaming scarlet letters in her brain.

What sort of lover would Tom Jamieson make?

Her mouth was dry, her heart fluttering frantically, knocking against her ribs in a panicked beat.

And then he was spinning her away and she could tell herself she'd imagined those heated seconds.

She refused to meet his eyes directly again, focussing anywhere else on his face. His mouth, the feral smile. Did he understand what she was doing? She would insist they take a break after this song so she could gather her tattered composure.

And then he was lifting her, the world tilted crazily for a second and then she was back on her feet, twirling away, only to be snatched back and dipped as Tom arched her over his arm.

The music stopped. She blinked up into hot chocolate eyes.

Applause and whistles filtered through her hazy thoughts.

He set her back on her feet and caught her hand in his as he grinned and sketched a brief bow to their audience.

Tom had controlled her easily, effortlessly, masterfully.

And she'd revelled in every moment of it.

'Let's have a coffee and then I'll see you home,' he said as the band announced they were taking a short break.

Catching her lip, she waged a silent battle. Common sense told her she needed to head home. She glanced at her watch. 'I'll take a rain-check on the coffee as it's nearly ten o'clock. Thank you for dinner and the dancing. It was wonderful.'

'I'll see you home.'

Her heart skittered. 'There's no need. I have the car.'

'I know. I'll follow you.'

Sensing the futility of arguing, she nodded. The sooner she got home, the sooner she'd be out of his disturbing orbit. She drove home, aware of his vehicle behind her for the brief journey.

His headlights loomed in her rear-vision mirror as she turned into her driveway. Keys ready, she got out of her car.

He met her on the path, taking her arm and walking her to her front door. He'd left his motor running, the steady chug of the diesel engine the only sound.

As she slid the key into the lock, she felt her hair being brushed aside, felt warm breath on her neck. Shuddered as his lips pressed to her nape, feeling the marrow in her bones turn to jelly.

'We could be good together, Kayla,' he said softly. 'I haven't given up the idea of pinning you down.'

She turned, wrapped her fingers around the strap of her shoulder bag to stop them from reaching for him. 'I'm not some hapless camp draft steer you can run around pegs in the arena.'

He leaned on the door, his hands bracketing her head. 'Honey, you'd be a heifer, not a steer and, trust me, I'd bypass the arena and take you straight to the branding yard if I could.'

It took a moment for his murmured words to sink in and then laughter bubbled up from somewhere deep inside her.

'I don't think I've met anyone quite like you, Tom Jamieson.'

She wiped moisture from beneath her eyes then lowered her hand to clutch her bag.

'I guess that's good.' His grin faded quickly. 'I like making you laugh. You should do it more often.'

He tilted his head and captured her lips. Just the barest touch of his clever mouth, warm, undemanding, almost waiting. She needed to step back but instead she felt herself begin to tremble, her breath coming in short, desperate gasps. Only then did his hands move to her face, to tip her head so he could deepen the kiss.

She was vaguely aware of a small thud as she dropped her bag and brought her hands up to cling to his shoulders. His arms came around her, scooping her even closer.

And then it was over.

He stepped back, lifting a hand to cup her jaw, his thumb stroked lightly across her mouth, making her aware of how swollen and pouty her lips felt. 'I won't give up, Kayla.'

'You should.' Shivers spiralled out of her stomach to every part of her body. 'Goodnight, Tom.'

She watched him go. The temptation to ask him in was nearly unbearable. She had to severely curtail the amount of time she spent with him before she did something they'd both regret. He made her feel things she'd never felt with a man before. A craving for his touch, his scent, his presence.

Being responsible had never seemed a heavier burden than it did right this minute.

CHAPTER ELEVEN

'Good morning, Hilda,' Kayla said cheerfully. She glanced at the waiting room as she joined the nurse at the emergency room status board. A woman was sipping from a mug with her arms around one child while a second sat sucking his thumb beside her. They all looked grubby and dazed. 'Looks like we're busy.'

'Kayla, you're early.' Hilda gave her a brief smile and pushed a stray hair back from her forehead with the back of her hand. The usually immaculate nurse looked subdued. 'Things are just settling down now. This is the first chance I've had to update the board.'

She could hear a deep, harsh coughing from the cubicle area as someone struggled to draw breath, then a man's raised, agitated voice.

'Fill me in. Who's our priority?'

'We've got smoke inhalation victims from a house fire. The Martin family. Tony's with the father now. The youngest child has been sedated and ventilated for airlift down to the Children's.'

'That's the rest of the family in the waiting room?'

'Yes, they've been checked over. The grandmother is on her way to pick up the kiddies. It could have been much worse if Tom Jamieson hadn't been passing their house.'

'Tom?' Kayla glanced at the board, her skin prickling with

apprehension. His name wasn't there. Relief settled like quivering jelly into her knees.

'He was the hero of the day.'

Was? *Was?* Kayla's heart stopped then lurched into motion again with a sickening, fluttery beat. Suddenly, *not* having Tom's name on the board *didn't* sound like good news.

'He woke the family, got them out and then went back in for the kiddie we're transferring.'

She was grateful when Hilda continued but she wanted to shake her and demand information about Tom. His name set up a persistent tattoo in her mind and she didn't trust herself to speak.

'The father went back in so Tom had to pull him out, too.'

Oh, God! Tom!

Kayla uncleaved her tongue from the roof of her dry mouth. 'Is he all right?'

'He's not good. That's him you can hear coughing.'

At least he's alive. Relief shuddered through her in a profound wave, leaving her shaky and weak. She put her hand on the wall to steady herself—as soon as she could trust her legs she was going to find him, see for herself that he was all right.

Hilda shook her head. 'The crazy things people do under pressure. His wife thinks he was after his coin collection.'

'Tom. I meant is Tom all right?' Kayla's throat felt raw and she was surprised when Hilda didn't seem to notice the croaky rasp.

'He's a bit knocked about but he seems okay. He's in cubicle three, waiting for Tony to finish.'

'I'll take a look at him now.'

'Oh, would you? That'd be great. I've been doing obs.' She glanced at the watch pinned to her uniform. 'He's due for another lot now.'

'I'll do them.' She walked on wobbly legs towards the area, barely holding her shudders of reaction in check.

She'd turned him down last night because of her fear of making a mistake, of losing control of her plans. He, on the other hand, was fearless, putting himself on the line, throwing himself, his precious life, into a dangerous situation.

All he'd asked her to do was to take a chance, go out with him. She'd drawn back, hesitant, afraid.

She felt barely able to contain the brew of conflicting emotions bubbling inside her. Anger with him for putting himself in danger and yet so achingly proud of him at the same time. He embraced life, the danger and mess and pain of it.

While she played it safe from the sidelines.

Sure, she planned on travelling north to work in remote areas. But in her usual careful way, she'd tried to ensure nothing deflected her from her course, nothing got untidy along the way.

As Tom had teased last night, she was even *rebelling with caution*. It suddenly seemed like a sad indictment of the person she was.

She slipped into the cubicle through the gap in the curtains.

Tom was sitting up on the bed, leaning back on the pillows, eyes closed. She was glad of this moment before he noticed her, so she could devour him with her eyes. She wanted to run to his side, slide her hands over every inch of him to make sure he really was all right. Hot tears gathered, pressing for release, but she blinked them back.

In a moment she would have to click into professional mode and work through his clinical examination but for a few precious seconds she could just look.

One leg bent with his forearm braced on the knee and his hand dangling. The other soot-smudged hand rested on the sheet, the clip of an oximeter attached to his finger.

His pale blue uniform shirt hung open. The fabric was

pockmarked with tiny cinder holes. On the sleeve, the upper arm badge was smeared with black, as were the white chevrons of his dark blue shoulder epaulettes. A long, ragged tear on the front panel just over Tom's ribs showed traces of blood. Where the edges of the shirt parted, a corner of gauze pad peeped out.

She must have made some small sound because his eyes snapped open and the dark-lashed brown gaze zeroed in on her. She felt as though she'd been zapped by a defibrillator. His whole demeanour changed.

'Kayla,' he rasped, his red-rimmed eyes sliding past her. 'What are you doing here?'

She made a superhuman effort to pull herself together. 'I've come to check you over.'

'I was expecting Tony.' He sat up, swinging his legs off the bed.

'He's busy.' She picked up his chart from the end of the bed and concentrated on his obs. BP slightly elevated, pulse normal, oxygen saturation normal. Shallow laceration. Calmer now, she hung the clipboard back on the rail.

'You get me instead.' She glanced at his face, noting the dirty smudges down one side. 'Is there a problem?'

'Hell, yes, there's a problem.' He scowled.

Her stomach swooped at his fierce look. When he didn't go on, she said, 'And that would be?'

'I want your hands on me, Kayla, but not in any damned professional capacity.' He unclipped the oximeter.

'Tom, you need—'

'You're not my doctor,' he said roughly as he stripped off the nasal cannula then stood in his socked feet and pulled the edges of his shirt together. 'I'm serious.'

'So am I.' She put her hand on his arm, felt the muscle twitch beneath warm skin. 'You're not going anywhere until you've been thoroughly checked over.' When he just looked at her silently, she said, 'And it doesn't make me your doctor.

Tony is the attending and I'll make sure he sees you and confirms everything I'm telling you.'

An unpleasant waft of stale smoke filled her nostrils, reminding her why they were there. 'Please, Tom, get back up on the bed.'

'As long as this isn't going to cause you any ethical dilemmas. If it will, you tell me now.' He gave her a narrow-eyed stare. 'I'll discharge myself rather than have you use it as *another* excuse to avoid what's between us.'

'Crabby when we're not well, are we?' she teased gently in an attempt to lighten the moment.

'I mean it, Kayla.' He was obviously in no mood to be cajoled into co-operation. 'Tell me if this is going to be a problem.'

'There's no dilemma.'

'What does that mean?' he growled.

'It means treating you now won't make you my patient. God knows, I wouldn't want anyone so difficult,' she said, goaded. 'And it won't change how I think of you.'

'Not quite what I wanted to hear but it'll do for now.' He gave her the slow, lopsided grin through the sooty daubs on his face. The poignancy of it pierced straight to her heart.

She swallowed hard and dredged up the tattered remnants of her exasperation. 'So sit down, shut up and take your blasted shirt off.'

'Great bedside manner, Dr Morgan.'

'Glad you like it. Less lip and more action from my patient would be even better.'

'Yes, Doc.' He moved slowly as though he ached.

'Let me help,' she said, reaching to peel the grimy garment carefully off his shoulders.

'If I'd realised running into a burning building would make you want to take my clothes off, I might have done it weeks ago.'

'Funny man.' She congratulated herself on her detachment as he pulled his arms out of the sleeves.

'Do you feel short of breath?' she said, feeling the constriction in her own breathing as he sat on to the edge of the bed, his shirt bunched in his hands.

'No.'

'Headache? Nausea?'

'No.'

She examined his eyes, peeling back the lids, all the time aware of his steady regard. Nose and throat—all the mucosal tissues were pink and healthy.

'Now I know how a horse feels, having a soundness check. Do I pass muster?' He lowered his voice. 'Will you want me? I won't cost you much.'

'Coming on to your doctor is poor form,' she said, hoping her desperation didn't show in the clipped words.

'But you're not my doctor.'

'Let's pretend I am for this exercise,' she muttered. Her hand was *not* going to tremble. She wouldn't let it. 'It'll make it easier on both of us.'

She unhooked her stethoscope from around her neck and put in the earpieces. 'I'm going to listen to your chest then I'll look at the laceration over your ribs. Just breathe normally for me.'

He gave her a quizzical look as she lifted the diaphragm and stepped beside him. The steady *lub-dub* of his heart was somewhat above normal rate—but, then, so was hers right now. After all *he'd* been through, it wasn't unexpected.

She closed her eyes and listened intently at each auscultation point for any abnormality in his lungs, any signs of fluid accumulation in the delicate respiratory tissues.

She reached around to his back and pressed the diaphragm into place, ignoring the toned muscle and warm skin beneath her fingertips.

'Okay, that sounds good.' She straightened and removed the stethoscope. 'Any tightness or pain when you breathe?'

'No. Just my ribs when I cough.'

'Let me take your shirt and I'll have a look now.' She held out her hands and he parted with it reluctantly. For the first time she noticed a long, narrow midline scar.

'You've had abdominal surgery.'

'Yes.' He obviously wasn't going to elaborate.

'How long ago?'

'A couple of years.'

'No ongoing issues?'

'No.'

She snapped on a pair of gloves and bent to peel back the dressing on his laceration. The wound was a shallow gouge, with bruising just starting to develop around the edges. But it was the small circular scar lower down, with its smooth centre and puckered edges, that held her rooted to the spot.

'You've been shot.'

'Oh, that.' He shifted, almost a wriggle as though he was embarrassed. 'Yeah.'

'How did it happen?'

'The usual way.'

'You've got a smart mouth, you know that?' She compressed her lips into a thin line, holding herself tightly in check. He could have been killed this morning. He could have been killed by this bullet. And all he could do was make light of it. His flippancy was the last straw. She wanted to smack him...she wanted wrap her arms around him, stop him from putting himself in harm's way.

But most of all...worst of all...she wanted to kiss him.

She took a deep, steadying breath and checked his back. No blemish. Not a through and through, then. A catalogue of the underlying structures flowed through her mind. A little higher or lower or further to the right and the outcome might have been very different. 'Is this related to your laparotomy?'

'Yes.'

'What damage did you sustain?'

'I lost a bit of large intestine apparently. I don't miss it.'

'You were lucky.'

'Yeah, I was,' he said softly.

She turned her attention to the recent damage.

'Take a deep breath for me, please. Any pain?'

'A bit.'

She reached out to press lightly on the ribs around the area. 'What about now?'

'Yes,' he hissed out through clenched teeth.

'I'm sorry. You've got some nasty bruising, if not a fractured rib.' She straightened. 'How did it happen?'

'Don fell on me when I was helping him out of the house. He was pretty groggy by the time I got to him. I landed on a lump on the floor with him on top of me. He's a big bloke.'

His laconic understatement told her more than anything else how fraught those moments in the burning building must have been.

'Did you hit your head when you fell?'

'No.'

'Okay. Lie down on the bed, I just want to check your abdomen and then we'll send you for an X-ray.'

As soon as she touched him, she felt his quick breath in. 'Just breathe normally. Don't hold.'

'Right. Breathe normally,' he muttered.

'That's better.' She moved her hand along the soft tissue below his ribcage, palpating gently.

He groaned.

'That hurt?' She froze, her fingers poised lightly on the upper abdominal quadrant. No guarding and it felt normal, but his response indicated otherwise.

'No.' He sounded strained, as though his teeth were clamped together. 'Have you finished?'

Lifting her hands and steepling her fingers, she said, 'So, no tenderness at all?'

'None.'

She frowned at him, noting the slash of red across his cheekbones. His gaze was fixed on the ceiling, his mouth set in a straight, hard line as though he was angry.

As Kayla turned away, she suppressed a sigh. 'I'll organise a dressing for that and then we'll get you down to Radiology.'

She worked in silence, irrigating the wound then drying the surrounding skin.

'After the X-ray, can I go?'

'I want you to stay here for a few hours so we can keep an eye on you,' she said as she squeezed some antiseptic ointment onto a non-stick dressing pad.

'No chance,' he said gruffly.

She taped the dressing in place and stifled the urge to berate him. Stripping off her gloves, she said, 'Let's get you X-rayed and then we'll see, depending on the results.'

'*Tony* will see,' he corrected.

She tipped her head in acknowledgement. 'Tony will see. If it's clear, you should take it easy for the rest of the day. No exertion. But you must come back or call an ambulance if you start having difficulty breathing, any headaches or nausea. Or if the hoarseness in your voice gets worse.'

'Got it.'

She made notes on his record sheet. 'Stay here. I'll arrange the X-ray and then get Tony to come and have a word.'

'Thanks, Kayla.'

She nodded and stepped out of the curtained cubicle. She straightened her shapeless hospital-issue white coat and took a deep breath. He was fine.

Fine. There was no need to have him admitted and put under twenty-four-hour observation. It would be a waste of resources.

And he'd never agree.

The hospital would never agree to having him forcibly detained for his own good, either.

But it was what she wanted to do.

Tom watched the curtain close behind Kayla, then tipped his head back onto the pillow and shut his eyes.

The sounds of the emergency department filtered into his consciousness. The deep hacking cough of the man he'd rescued, the subdued murmur of staff. A beeper sounding.

Today's Kayla was all business in her white coat of armour with her stethoscope and clinical detachment. The silver-grey eyes had been steady and assessing. Her touch gentle but impersonal. Hard to take when he yearned for so much more.

No sign of the woman whose lips had burned under his and shaken him to the core. No sign of the magical, fluid creature who'd been so sweetly responsive to his lead on the dance floor less than twenty-four hours ago.

He'd looked for a glimpse of caring, for something personal over and above her professional manner. But apart from that fleeting moment of dismay when she'd identified his old bullet wound and a couple of small slips where her irritation had showed, she'd been cool and efficient.

He'd been nothing more than a job to her.

Last night, she'd told him in no uncertain terms that he was wasting his time. But he'd still come away with her kisses on his lips and felt hopeful.

Now he just felt tired and battered. Dispirited. His ribs hurt, the skin over them stung—but worst of all was the ache in his heart.

Later in the morning, Kayla saw Tony at the desk.

'Have you heard how our house-fire victims are?' She picked up the results of the biochemistry work-up she'd requested on a diabetic patient.

'Father and son both on ventilators but they're stable.'

'And Tom?' She'd already checked his X-ray but perhaps Tony had picked up something she'd missed.

'Tom?' Tony sounded vague, his mind obviously on the file he was reading. 'He's fine. I discharged him after checking his X-ray.'

'No problems, then?'

Her boss looked up from the folder in his hand, his shrewd eyes fixing on her. 'Like what?'

'Nothing in particular,' she said, wishing she hadn't persisted. 'His rib was very tender, I just wondered.'

Tony shrugged and went back to his reading. 'Heavy bruising. I went through his home care. Which I gather you'd already covered.' He flipped the page. 'And I told him to come back at the first sign of any problems—which you'd also covered.'

'Good. Thanks.'

His lack of concern should have been reassuring. She didn't need to follow up further, didn't need to go out to Tom's place to check up on him.

But she wanted to...

CHAPTER TWELVE

KAYLA slowed to a halt at the front of the burnt-out house, her stomach clenching. Tom had been in there while hungry flames wreaked their havoc. He'd gone in twice, *twice*, heedless of the risk to himself to pull out the occupants.

A cold chill shivered down her spine as she stared at the charred roof struts poking out of gaping holes where the roof tiles had fallen in. The front entrance was an open, smoke-stained mouth with broken windows like sightless eye sockets on either side. She could see all the way through the blackened interior of the house to the rose glow of sunset-etched plants in the back yard.

Jack had told Liz the smoke detectors hadn't had batteries. The family was lucky to be alive.

And so was Tom.

She swallowed the nausea that threatened to rise up her throat.

Her pulse thumped in a quick rhythm. Each beat mocked her interest in the house as the procrastination it really was.

She was afraid.

Tom seemed so sure of what he wanted. Her stomach swooped sickeningly. He pushed her out of her comfort zone just by being himself. What if he expected more than she had to give, more than she was capable of?

She swallowed. She couldn't let herself think about that

now. Tonight she was here to check on his recovery, cook him dinner, make a gesture. Not seduce him.

He was right. She was in Dustin, she was involved with the town. With him. But she could choose the level of the involvement.

With one final look, she put the car in gear. Tom's place was further along on the outer fringes of the township. She'd only been there the once, on Friday night…only a couple of days ago. But the way she felt, it could have been a lifetime ago with all that had happened since.

She parked on the gravel in front of Tom's house and gathered the handles of the shopping bags with trembling fingers.

He'd said he liked steak so she'd bought eye fillet and vegetables. And sticky date pudding. She chewed her lip. Had she brought too much? Overdone it? She blew out an impatient breath and scrambled out of the car. The bags weren't heavy but with each step closer to the house they seemed to gain unbelievable weight. If she kept this up, she was going to paralyse herself with doubt.

She marched up the steps to knock on the front door before she could change her mind.

Keep it light. Keep it light. Keep it—

The door opened and suddenly Tom was there.

Her heart ricocheted around her ribcage before lodging in her throat as she stared at him. Powerful shoulders and arms were left bare by the navy singlet that moulded to his torso. She could see the outline of the dressing she'd applied to his ribs earlier. Faded blue jeans rode low on his hips.

'Kayla.' His voice, still slightly hoarse from the smoke he'd inhaled, was flat.

She jerked her eyes back up to meet his narrow-eyed stare. He looked moody and his mouth had firmed to a thin uncompromising line.

She swallowed. He was fine, more than fine.

But he was far from pleased to see her. She hadn't really expected that. An unpleasant band tightened around her heart. Perhaps she should have called first.

'I came to see how you were.' If anything, he looked even grimmer. *Keep it light.* She held up her shopping bags as though they were offerings to appease. 'And I brought dinner. You cooked for me the other night—I thought I'd return the favour tonight.'

He moved aside silently.

She walked into the foyer and waited while he closed the door. His face was unreadable as he held out his hands for the bags.

'Oh, no. They're not heavy,' she said, clutching the handles. Her smile felt uncomfortable; a desperate, flimsy disguise for her fear of rejection. 'I'll…take them through to the kitchen if that's okay?'

'Sure. Why not?'

Her smile faltered. So far from the welcome she'd hoped for but at least he'd let her in. The temptation to turn tail in the face of his gruffness was nearly overwhelming. He didn't want her there—he couldn't be any clearer. She would make him dinner and leave as quickly as possible.

'Right.' She turned and began to walk.

Although he moved silently, she was aware of him every step of her journey along the wide hall. She knew the moment he stopped at the kitchen doorway while she continued across the room.

She moved behind the island bench. Having Tom nearby seemed more manageable now that she had the barrier between them. She lifted the bags on the bench and pulled out the carrots, greens and onions. 'You said you preferred steak so that's what I've brought. Do you have a barbecue?' She glanced over to where he stood with his thumbs hooked into the belt band of his jeans. 'Or should I do it under the griller?'

'I've got a barbecue.'

'Well, don't light it yet.' Not that he'd offered. Unhappiness knotted her stomach as she looked down at the vegetables on the bench. The sooner she got on with this the sooner she could go. She squared her shoulders and, with determined brightness she said, 'I've gone for comfort food.' She looked around while she spoke then glanced at him. 'Is it okay if I raid your drawers for a peeler?'

He shrugged, looking cool and disinterested. 'Raid them for whatever you like.'

She found a small peeler then set to work on a carrot. The silence was unbearable. She had to fill it—even if it was with ramblings. 'I'm going to make a stir-fry. I hope you like asparagus. I couldn't resist it. The supermarket had a fresh batch.'

The flow of words took on a life of their own now that she'd started. She shrugged mentally as she heard herself start about the sticky date pudding for desert. If he wasn't going to contribute or deflect her ramblings then he'd just have to make of it whatever he liked.

She paused for a breath, searching for another topic.

'Why are you here, Kayla?' He sounded tired.

Her heart lurched. She should have known once he did break his silence, he'd cut straight to the chase. He was going to make her work for this. She could feel her courage slipping away.

'I told you, I came to see how you are.' She flashed him a quick smile. Desperate to keep working with her hands, she twisted around to rummage in the drawer for a knife. 'So how are you?'

She straightened and turned. A small gasp locked in her throat. Tom stood a scant foot from her. Her fingers clenched around the handle of the utensil she held.

His darkly lashed eyes moved over her face then slipped downwards. She followed his line of vision to the paring knife she held in front of her as though she was preparing to defend her honour. He reached out to unfurl her fingers.

With the blade safely on the bench, he folded his arms. 'Are you asking me as a doctor? Or a friend? Or something else?'

'A f-friend.'

Tom clenched his jaw to stop the pithy word that sprang to his tongue.

She was here as a friend with her food and succour and medical expertise.

All he wanted was her.

Just her. Plain and simple.

And so bloody complex.

He curled his fingers into fists. 'Well, *friend*, you didn't pick a great time. I'm not feeling all that...friendly at the moment.'

She winced and looked away. A flash of vulnerability in her eyes cut straight to his heart and he regretted his sharp tone.

'Then...how about as a woman who h-has changed her mind?'

His unruly heart skipped a beat before common sense insisted he was probably misunderstanding her. 'Changed her mind about what?' he asked evenly.

'Getting involved.' Her words came out haltingly as though she was forcing each one off her tongue. 'With. You.'

His whole body shook with the need to reach out to grab her. Jerking away, he stalked across the room. Hell. The woman he craved was standing here in his kitchen, apparently offering herself to him on a platter. *But why now?* He didn't like the answer that presented itself.

He turned back to face her. 'Is this some sort of warped hero-worship thing?'

Her mouth dropped open. 'No! Of course not.' She made a small negative movement with her hands then clasped them in front of her. 'I mean you are a hero but that's not why I'm here.'

He watched her, not trusting himself to get closer. 'Then why now?'

'You're not going to make this easy, are you?' She put her hands on the bench behind her as though to steady herself. He could see her tension in the way each finger gripped, her skin stretched white across each knuckle. She stared at the floor, gnawing at her bottom lip as though to gather courage.

He ran a hand over his face—he wanted her but he didn't want her coming to him as some sort of misguided self-sacrifice. It wouldn't be right. Besides, he wanted her to want *him*. Just him, not some heroic version she thought he was.

'All right.' As though she'd made a decision, she looked up. Grey eyes burned into his with a dark intensity that took his breath away. 'Right from the first time I laid eyes on you, you scared me to death. I'm afraid of the way you make me feel.'

He could feel the heat burning in his face. This was the third time she'd made him blush. 'How do I make you feel?'

'As though I'm out of control.' The tip of her tongue made a quick, nervous sweep of her lips and he felt his system jolt. 'You're larger than life and I...don't know if I can handle you.'

'Handle me?'

Her eyes clung to his. 'I've never felt anything like this and it terrifies me. Y-you terrify me.'

'God, Kayla,' he groaned. He was torn. Half of him wanted to take her in his arms, reassure her, seduce her until she accepted the magic of the chemistry between them. The other half of him wondered if his long-term plans would be better served by halting her flow of words until he had the composure to deal with her confession. 'What am I going to do with you?'

The colour came and went in her face. 'Nothing, by the

sounds of it.' She huffed out a small self-mocking laugh that ended in a hiccup. 'You've changed your mind, haven't you?'

'Changed my mind? No, I haven't changed my mind,' he rasped. 'I've been frustrated for the entire two months, three weeks and roughly six days since you arrived in Dustin.'

She blinked. 'R-really?'

'Oh, yeah.' He smiled ruefully, still not trusting himself to go near her.

She caught her bottom lip between her teeth for a moment. 'W-well, where does that leave us, then?'

'I know what I want.' He speared his fingers through his hair, continuing the thrust until his hand reached the back of his neck. 'I don't know what you want and I'm worried you don't know, either. I know I suggested I could become part of your rebellion. But you refused me last night, Kayla. The only thing that's happened since then is the fire.'

'I know.' She looked at him steadily. 'Finding out you were in the emergency department this morning gave me a shock. Made me realise how fragile life is.' Her throat moved in a swallow. 'How important you are. And how right you were last night. I am involved here in Dustin.'

'But I—'

She held her hand up. 'Please, Tom, let me finish. I want to be braver. I want to take some chances, do some things spontaneously.' She looked at him, her eyes dark pewter with emotion. 'I want…you.'

For a second he was frozen, his body paralysed by the intensity of his emotion. Then, in four strides, he was across the kitchen to scoop her face into his hands. 'I don't know if is the right thing but, heaven help me, I can't resist you.'

Her breathing changed, a tiny hitch…the most sexy thing. 'I'm glad. I've never thrown myself at a man before.'

'Is that what you're doing?' He kissed the corner of her mouth. 'Then I'm glad, too.' Another small peck in the centre of her mouth. 'A smart man would catch you and keep you.' Tom nibbled the cushion of her lower lip. He pulled back and looked down into her shining quicksilver eyes. 'I'm a smart man, Kayla.'

'Please. Kiss me again.' Her voice was a husky murmur, entrancing. Her lashes lowered as her eyes drifted down to his mouth. As potent as a touch. 'Let's worry about right now.'

Alarm bells jangled but not enough to still the need rising through him with a savagery he'd never felt before. He couldn't help himself. She was here, saying the things he wanted to hear. He couldn't say no. Couldn't.

Her hands clutched at his waist, then burrowed under his singlet to slide up. The feeling of her fingers on his skin was bliss.

He sucked in a deep breath and she stilled. 'Oh, your rib. Did that hurt?'

He could have laughed. Was she serious? 'Honey, trust me when I tell you that I'm feeling no pain right now.'

'Yes, but as your doctor—' He pressed his thumbs gently to her mouth, refusing to let her finish that sentence. He wanted her to see him as a man, not a patient. The soft, warm lips yielded beneath his touch.

'Not my doctor,' he said hoarsely as the tip of her tongue touched the sensitive pads of his fingers.

She smiled slowly and gave him a knowing look. 'Then as your lover-to-be, who happens to be a doctor, I feel honour-bound to point out that you're full of dopamine and other feel-good chemicals. You might be sorry you exerted yourself later.'

'I'll never regret this.' He touched his lips to hers. 'Never.'

CHAPTER THIRTEEN

'I THINK you might be a bad influence,' Kayla murmured. Beneath her ear, Tom's heart beat a rapid tattoo that synchronised with her stuttering pulse. She lay boneless, half-sprawled across his chest, so completely exhausted and relaxed she wondered when she'd be able to move again.

Or if she'd ever want to. She smiled at the fanciful thought of staying right where she was—listening to the rhythm of a man's heartbeat. Not just any man—specifically Tom Jamieson.

'Bad influence? Who? Me?' His fingers traced lazy patterns up and down her arm.

'Yes, you.' She inhaled his fragrance—hot, male and musky. Delicious. 'I don't think I've ever felt so...wicked.' She paused. 'I think I like it.'

'Stick with me, honey. I'll show you everything I know.' Rich amusement threaded through his voice.

She brushed her hand through the dark hair on his chest, enjoying the feel of it on the sensitive skin of her palm. 'Promise?'

His arm tightened, holding her even closer as his laughter vibrated through his torso and into her body. 'And you were worried about being able to handle me.'

She swallowed, gathering her courage. 'I—I think I'll take you up on your offer if it's still open.'

'I'll be happy to oblige.' His voice rumbled under her ear in instant agreement. Her heart skipped. A small pause and then he said, 'Which offer was that?'

She tweaked a couple of chest hairs in a light tug, feeling half foolish, half annoyed. 'How can you say you'll be happy to oblige if you can't even remember what it's about?'

'Ouch.' He captured her fingers and carried them to his lips. 'Hey, if it involves you and me together, how can I lose?'

He sounded so sincere and certain. The unexpected, unconditional support caught her on the raw.

'Nice recovery,' she said huskily around the hot lump that had formed in her throat.

'I thought so.' After a small silence, he said, 'What have I committed to?'

She took a steadying breath. 'To being part of my Dustin rebellion.'

'Oh, yeah.' The warmth in his voice made her toes curl. 'I'm at your command.'

She propped herself up on one elbow and looked down at him. 'You sound like you're about to offer me three wishes.'

His fingers curled around the back of her neck. 'Honey, you can have as many wishes as you like.'

He tugged her mouth down to his.

'Can I have that in writing?' she said, feeling his lips curve under hers.

He caught her lower lip gently between his teeth for a moment. 'You'll have to take it on trust.'

She pulled back, averting her eyes from his. His words were teasing but they instantly doused the glow that had warmed her heart.

She could feel his gaze on her profile, could sense his curiosity about her withdrawal. To distract him, and herself, she ran her hand across his flat belly, felt his sharply indrawn breath as his muscles contracted beneath her fingertips.

She traced the thin flat laparotomy scar then detoured to the nubbly little scar near his flank.

'Tell me what happened.'

'It was a carjacking.' His voice was gravelly. He cleared his throat. 'One in a series of attacks. The guy waited in railway car parks, preying on young women as they came out of the station to their cars.'

'I think I remember,' she said slowly, searching her memory for the details. 'He made them drive to deserted locations then raped them and took their cars.'

'That's right. He was getting bolder. The violence of his attacks was escalating.'

'He shot the off-duty policeman who stopped him.' She looked into the steady, dark eyes watching her. 'That was you.'

'Yeah. I was lucky. He had a point two-two air pistol.'

She raised her eyebrows. 'That's lucky?'

'Solid pellet, no fragmentation.'

'You could still have been killed,' she said severely, to cover the fear that cramped her stomach. How could he think about the technicalities when his life had been at stake?

'But I wasn't.' He brushed her hair back, tucking it behind her ear.

'You're a hero.' A blush swept across his cheekbones, fascinating her.

He shook his head. 'Just someone doing what they had to at the time.'

'It's more than a lot of people would have done. Same with the house fire this morning.' She examined his face, feature by feature. The regular, lean, good looks hid a lion's heart. 'You're a very special man.'

'I'm not sure where you're going with this, Kayla.' Dark eyes glittered intently up at her as he tilted his head on the pillow and frowned. 'But I'm not special. Cut me and I bleed. I hurt just like any other man.'

A spiral of icy discomfort twisted through her gut and she had to look away.

Regardless of his modesty, he was courageous, physically and emotionally. So open and loving and family orientated. She was none of those things—for all that she had envied her friends with close family. Was there something missing in her, some integral ingredient, that meant she had to be on the outside?

And where did that leave Tom? Would she hurt him before they were done? She had to be careful that didn't happen.

'What's wrong?'

'Nothing.' She smiled, feeling the stiffness of her face. 'Hey, I promised you food.'

'Kayla—'

She moved away to scramble off the other side of the bed. 'Mind if I use your shower?'

'Sure.' He propped himself up on one elbow. 'There's a clean towel in the cupboard beside the door.'

'And the bathroom?'

'Across the passage.'

As she walked to the door, his eyes were irresistibly drawn down her trim back, the curve of her waist, over the flare of peach-shaped buttocks to long legs.

His pulse revved but he tamped down the stirrings of male interest.

Had she just run out on him?

He rolled off the bed, feeling his bruised ribs protesting the movement. Not so painless now, but he wouldn't change a thing about the last hour. In fact, given half a chance, he was ready to do it all over again.

Perhaps in the shower…

But when he got to the bathroom, Kayla had finished. The towel wrapped around her body was secured sarong-style above her breasts and covering way too much skin…but he could work with it.

She met his eyes in the mirror. 'All yours.'

'Yes, please.' He stepped behind her, pressing his mouth to her nape. Satisfaction poured through him at her shiver.

'I didn't mean that.' Her throaty voice made him want to growl.

'Maybe you should have.' He reached out and caught the towel. 'Kayla?'

She didn't resist as he turned her to face him. When he bent to touch his lips to hers, she brought her hands up to frame his face. He contemplated the logistics of making love in the shower cubicle, the idea growing on him by the second.

The next moment he was free, a damp towel dangling from his hand.

'Don't dawdle,' she said over her shoulder as she waltzed out the door towards his bedroom. 'I'll go and finish preparing the vegetables.'

On the surface, she was all beans and business but he couldn't help wondering if it was clever camouflage for something that had upset her. He tightened his grip on the towel, tempted to follow her and pin her to the bed until he got to the bottom of whatever it was.

'I'll get you to turn on the barbecue plate for the steak when you come out.' Kayla's voice floated cheerily across the hallway.

He shook his head, telling himself he must have imagined that moment of coolness. Stepping into the shower cubicle, he reached for the taps. He washed quickly making sure he kept the dressing over his ribs as dry as possible. It was waterproof but he figured the less he disturbed it for today the better.

Back in the bedroom he pulled on a clean pair of boxers, dragged on his jeans, then padded along to the kitchen.

When he reached the archway, the domestic scene stopped him in his tracks. Without a trace of self-consciousness, Kayla was talking to a black and white cat sitting on the floor beside her.

Oh, yes, this was what he wanted, every day for the rest of his life.

This woman.

In his home.

In his heart.

He tucked his hands in his pockets as he walked across the tiles. 'I see Jerry's chatting you up.'

'His name's Jerry? Wasn't there a cartoon…?' She trailed off.

'*Tom and Jerry.* Naming him was Dad's idea. Too many comics when he was growing up.'

She chuckled.

'He's not usually this friendly.' Tom moved behind her and placed his hands on her waist, trapping her at the bench. 'You've charmed all the males in this household.'

'I think it's much more prosaic than that. I think the males here like their chances of getting what they want.'

'Uh-huh.' He nuzzled into the side of her neck. 'What are the chances?'

'Zero until after dinner.' She was proud of how steady her voice was given the quivers that zinged along her nerve pathways. His lips on her skin were electric. Before she could stop herself, she'd tilted her head, giving him better access to her nape. 'M-maybe we can renegotiate then.'

His hands flexed on her hips. 'I bet I could change your mind.'

'No bet.' She twisted out of his grip. In a smooth movement, she scooped up the plate that held the steaks and thrust it towards him. 'Be useful. Go and cook. Got to keep your strength up.'

'Good point.' He gave her a slow, wicked smile. 'How do you like your steak?'

'Medium.'

She blew out a long, shaky breath as he moved away. With him safely outside, she raised a hand to her sternum. Her flesh trembled with each hard beat of her heart. Turning back to the bench, she stood staring at the vegetables. She was out of her depth but the temptation to keep trying to stay afloat with Tom was overwhelming.

'Problem?'

She jumped, her heart lurching out of rhythm. 'No. No problem. Are you…?' Her mind went completely blank for a long moment. 'Um, have you got any soy sauce?'

'In the pantry in the corner.'

'Great.' She reached for the door handle. 'I don't suppose you have a wok?'

'You'd be wrong. It's in the cupboard under the sink.' He peered under the island bench and after a moment held up a bottle. 'Red wine?'

'A half-glass would be nice. Thanks.' The vegetables would only take a couple of minutes. She put the pan on a moderate heat then turned back to face Tom.

With a few expert twists of his wrist, he had the cork removed from the bottle. He moved with grace, economy and confidence. She liked watching him—more than was sensible. The sturdy wrists. Firm, well-muscled biceps, not too bulky. Forearms lightly covered with dark hair. The plain silver watch strapped above his left wrist shouldn't have been sexy…but it was.

He set the bottle aside with the glasses to breathe. 'I'll go and turn the steak.'

Glad to have something to do, Kayla tipped the vegetables into the wok, stirring the heat through them.

A short time later, they were seated at the table. The same makeshift candle holders glowed in the centre of the table.

Tom poured wine into the glasses then handed her one and chinked the lip of his against hers.

'A toast to rebellion,' he said, smiling at her mischievously over the rim of his glass.

Her cheeks warmed.

'To rebellion.' She lifted her drink and took a sip.

'I'm glad you came to check up on me tonight. Thanks,' he said softly.

The warm gratitude in his eyes made her want to fidget. She slid the casserole dish across the table. 'My pleasure. Help yourself before it cools down.'

Tom picked up the serving spoon, added a scoop of stir-fried vegetables to his plate and turned the conversation to more general topics. He sensed Kayla's relief and he was rewarded when she relaxed again and opened up more. Her warm laughter rolled over him.

As he looked his fill, he reflected how well she fitted, with him, with his life.

It was much later when she pushed back her chair and picked up the plates. 'We'd better clear up. How about I wash since I don't know where things go?'

He liked it that she sounded as regretful as he was that there was no excuse to linger at the table.

'Sure.' He picked up the serving dish and glasses and followed her to the sink. 'I'm going to my cousin's engagement party on Saturday night. Want to come?'

'Your cousin? Didn't I meet him and his girlfriend at the camp draft barbecue?'

'Jonathon and Natalie,' he confirmed.

'Sounds like fun. I'm working during the day but as long as everything's under control it should be okay.' Her voice was muffled as she rummaged under the bench. She came up with an ancient pair of dish-washing gloves he didn't know were there. 'I can take a change of clothes to work with me.'

'Great.' Congratulating himself on how well his casual approach was working, he went back to the table and snuffed out the candles. 'What about next week?'

'What about it?' she said over the running water.

'Here's how it works.' Back in the kitchen, he snagged a clean tea-towel from a drawer. 'Me plus you plus relationship equals me wanting to see you as often as possible.' With his hands busy wiping a glass, he studied her profile, trying to read her reactions. 'Every day would be good but I can be flexible.'

'Oh.' She washed the steak knives and put them on the drainer. Her lips pursed. Not a good sign. 'Next week, I'm studying because Saturday week I'm going down to Melbourne to do a course.' She lifted a plate out of the soapy water and slotted it into the rack, then hesitated. 'And I'll be staying down there.'

'You can study here.'

'Study here?' She glanced at him, as she stacked the second plate, her eyes filled with humour. 'With you around? I don't think so.'

'I can control myself.'

'Yes...well...maybe it's not you I'm worried about,' she muttered.

He threw the tea-towel on the rack and reached for her. 'You can't say things like that and expect to just stand there, washing dishes.'

She squeaked as he scooped her up, suds flying. Pain stabbed him in the side and he couldn't suppress a small grimace.

'Your ribs—' she began, her silver eyes shadowed with concern.

'Are fine as long as you stay still,' he said.

She frowned, but other than that she didn't move a muscle. 'They're not. I can see you've hurt yourself. Please, put me down.'

'Not on your life.' He turned and started for the door. 'I've got you where I want you.'

'Where are you taking me?'

'Back to the bedroom.' He smiled in anticipation.

'Tom,' she protested on a half-laugh. 'What about the rest of the dishes?'

'They'll still be there tomorrow.'

She held her green-covered fingers up. 'Then what about the gloves?'

'Maybe I like you in rubber.'

'Kinky.' She chuckled. The sound was delightful.

'Okay, so maybe not dishwashing gloves.' He turned and walked the short distance to the bench. 'Take them off.'

'Ooh, you're doing masterful.' She obediently dropped the gloves on the bench. 'It suits you.'

'You bet. Now you put your arms around my neck.'

She wound her arms around his neck and stroked his skin. He nearly moaned.

'Turn out the lights,' he growled as he stopped by the doorjamb.

In the bedroom, he pinned her to the bed. 'Now I've really got you where I want you.'

Where she belonged.

It was too soon to tell her that, of course, but he could show her, worship her with his body. Prove to her that they had something special.

After a magical hour of exploring each other, testing their limits, he wrapped her in his arms. Perfect. With her legs entwined with his like this, she had no chance of running out on him. As he drifted off to sleep, he smiled. He was looking forward to waking her up in the morning.

He woke slowly, in the filtered dawn light, aware of a pervasive sense of well-being. The warmth of a body was pressed to his torso.

Kayla. She was still here.

He reached down to stroke her awake.

Fur!

He sat bolt upright and pain stabbed him sharply in the side. Smothering a curse, he held a hand to his injured ribs and stared into Jerry's yellow eyes.

Kayla was gone.

Hours ago by the feel of the rest of the bed. The only warmth was that under Jerry's contented furry self.

Tom scowled. Kayla had run out on him after all.

If she thought that was acceptable, then she had another thought coming.

He threw back the covers and rolled out of bed. He had places to go...and a certain person to see.

CHAPTER FOURTEEN

As soon as he entered the kitchen, he saw the note propped up on the counter. So she hadn't *quite* done a runner on him. His simmering frustration eased a fraction.

He picked up the note, hoping for something to salve his bruised heart. Her writing, the little there was of it, was neat and controlled—like Kayla herself. Each beautifully formed letter sloped the same way. The words themselves were simple, concise. Bland. No acknowledgement of what had happened between them, nothing about their earth-shattering connection.

He smoothed the note on the bench, his eyes narrowing. Not even a damned X to signify a kiss.

Just that she'd see him tomorrow. It was something...but it wasn't much. It didn't come close to what he wanted.

He huffed out a breath, cautioning himself to be patient. She'd taken a huge step by coming to him last night, being prepared to admit that she wanted him. He had to take one careful step at a time. But if she thought leaving a note meant she was completely off the hook until tomorrow night, she was very much mistaken. A lazy smile spread across his face.

Later today, he'd find a way to see her—even if it was just briefly.

All the chairs in the emergency department were empty when Tom walked through the entrance that evening. Probably the lull before the evening rush. Good, he wouldn't be interrupting her.

'Hi, Hilda.' He leaned on the counter. 'Is Kayla about?'

'She's on a meal break while we're quiet.' The matronly nurse gave him a kind smile as though she could see through his casual demeanour. 'She shouldn't be long.'

'Down in the cafeteria?'

'As far as I know.'

'Thanks. I'll try and catch her there.' Anticipation hummed through his body. With luck, she'd be there alone.

He spotted his quarry at the sink, rinsing her mug. His gut tightened. A quick sweep confirmed the rest of the room was empty. Eyes focussed on Kayla, he stalked silently towards her.

When he was halfway across the room, her head whipped around sharply as though she sensed his presence. Her face lit up with a smile and his pulse leapt in response.

He wondered what she saw in his expression because a moment later her smile faltered. A wash of delicate colour swept across her fair skin. She turned to face him, clutching the mug in front of her breasts like a shield.

'Tom?'

'Kayla.'

He planted his hands on the bench either side of her and bent to capture her mouth. She tasted of coffee and dark chocolate. Tantalising. Sensational. He took his time, savouring the flavours, lingering over the warmth and softness of her lips. He heard her breath catch then quicken.

By a superhuman effort he kept the caress leisurely, ignoring his body's demand to plunge deeper. He tightened his grip on the bench, felt the fine tremors in his muscles from the self-control he exerted.

He drew back slowly and looked down into her wide eyes. The pupils had expanded into huge pools of black rimmed by quicksilver. 'Good morning.'

She blinked. 'Morning?'

'Yeah. I've been saving that for you *all* day.' His voice was rough with betraying emotion but he didn't care. 'Ever since I found you'd gone when I woke up.'

'Oh.' Her eyes flicked away and then back to him. 'I left you a note.'

'I saw it but it's not quite the same. Besides, there was no kiss in your note.' He deliberately slid his eyes down to her mouth. 'I had to rectify that oversight.'

She made a tiny sound, almost a whimper, as he leaned down to kiss her again.

Her lips clung to his but when he lifted his head, she stuttered, 'Y-you have to stop. I'm working.'

'I know. I'll get out of your hair now that I've finished making my special delivery.'

'R-right.' She looked adorable when she was flustered. 'Thanks.'

'You're very welcome.' He ran a finger across the cushion of her lower lip, feeling the faint dampness. The touch was a mistake, cranking his hunger almost beyond tolerance. He had to leave before he disgraced himself and begged her to let him stay with her tonight. 'Maybe you'll stay around to collect the next good-morning kiss in person. Not that I object to hunting you down to deliver them.'

He managed a smile. 'Goodnight, sweetheart. I hope you're not too busy tonight. I'll see you tomorrow.'

Kayla swallowed.

'See you then,' she rasped, barely able to recognise her voice.

He strode across the room, long legs eating the distance. Kayla caught her bottom lip between her teeth. Watching him move, watching everything about him, was a wayward pleasure that she didn't think would ever pall. From the short, dark hair on his well-shaped head, the broad shoulders stretching his plain white T-shirt, to the snug-fitting blue jeans. She'd never been so acutely conscious of a man's body before. Making love with him last night hadn't taken any of the edge off her awareness—if anything, it had made it more intense.

He stopped at the door to look back at her. The cocky smile that touched his lips sent her heart rate careening again.

As soon as he disappeared, she let out the breath that had frozen in her lungs and slumped back against the bench. A belated check of the room showed that no one had witnessed the scene. Tom knocked her sideways, making her forget her usual caution.

She shook herself mentally and turned to put her mug in the staff cupboard. Making a quick detour to the bathroom on her way back to the department, she checked her appearance. She looked the same as ever. No indelible scarlet stamp across her features that said *Tom Jamieson's lover*. The only clues anything out of the ordinary had happened in her meal break were her pink cheeks and uncontrollable smile. She set her mouth but the fatuous curve kept breaking through.

Hilda looked up as she re-entered the department. 'Did Tom find you?'

'Yes, he did,' Kayla said, her mind scrambling. She needed to think of something to say to change the subject. No way could she stand here and chat casually about Tom Jamieson. Her mind stayed unhelpfully blank.

'I see he's had no ill-effects after yesterday's events,' Hilda said.

Kayla stared at her blankly, heat spreading up through her body. Her affair with Tom couldn't be public knowledge…it couldn't. A wave of nausea cramped in her stomach.

Hilda raised her eyebrows then said, 'After the house fire.'

'Oh. Mmm.' Kayla sucked her lips in and clamped them between her teeth. If she opened her mouth, the first sound out was going to be laughter, and she didn't trust it not to be liberally tinged with hysteria.

'The wee one and his father are both off ventilators now. It was a close call.'

'Yes, it was.' The urge to laugh abruptly subsided in a shiver as Kayla remembered the burnt-out husk of the house and Tom's rescue of the family. He was a hero.

'Anyway, I've got a nasty set of tonsils in cubicle three for you,' Hilda said briskly. 'And a lacerated hand in two. Nineteen-year-old male, put his hand through a window.'

'Okay. Thanks.' She took the files, relieved to have something concrete to do.

If she and Tom went out, talk would be expected in a small town like Dustin. But that was different from everyone knowing that she was sleeping with him. She was an intensely private person so how did she feel about that being public knowledge?

How would Tom feel about it?

'You're very quiet. Is something wrong?' Tom glanced at Kayla as he steered along his driveway after his cousin's engagement party.

'No, I'm just pleasantly tired.' She paused then said, 'Jon and Natalie are lovely. They're good together.'

'They are.' Could he hear wistfulness in her voice—or was it only wishful thinking on his part?

He switched off the engine and unbuckled his seat belt. Turning towards her, he casually laid his arm across the back of the seats. He sifted his fingers through the gold silk of her hair. 'Want to make out in the car?'

She laughed and rolled her head to look at him. Light from the front porch caught in her eyes, showing the delicate spokes of silver radiating out from the pupils. 'You're a real romantic, you know that?'

'I'm taking my job as co-conspirator in your rebellion seriously.' He rubbed his jaw with his free hand. 'I can't help you with the whisker burn because I shaved earlier but I can definitely manage a love bite.'

'I'll pass on the whisker burn *and* the love bite but I'm very impressed with your dedication to your role.' She batted her eyelashes at him and grinned cheekily. 'I'm sure you've got other good ideas.'

'Yeah.' He cupped her jaw and ran his thumb across the soft, warm skin of her cheek. 'Stay.'

She turned her head and kissed the palm of his hand. 'Of course.'

'No, I meant stay the whole night. I want to wake up with you beside me.'

'Oh.' The smile faded from her eyes and she looked at him silently. 'I don't know if that's a good idea.'

'Why not?'

'I'm… It seems too hot and heavy for where we are. And I'm only here for a short time.'

'You've told me.' He examined her face, looking for a weakness, some indication he wasn't being a complete fool. They had something special, something worth giving a chance. He weighed his words with care. 'Let's get some things straight. We *are* hot and heavy. This might be a rebellion but it's also a relationship.'

'For the time I'm here.'

He clenched his jaw, feeling the grind of his molars as he held back the temptation to push. 'For the time you're here. Exclusive. Dating no one else.'

She was silent for a long, torturous moment. 'Aren't you worried what people will think?' Her sombre grey eyes held mixed emotions, the foremost being concern. For him.

'They'll think I got lucky.' He grinned but she didn't respond. His stomach dropped.

'I'm serious, Tom.'

'Why would they care?'

'You...have an important position in a small community.'

'And your point is?'

'People look up to you. Surely it's even more vital for you to maintain your reputation now than when you worked in the city.'

'How would you staying the night with me affect that?'

'You think I'm being ridiculous.' She chewed on her lip. 'I...guess...worrying about how things might be perceived is ingrained.' She stared through the windscreen but he had the feeling she wasn't seeing anything. She was too wrapped up in her thoughts.

Tom waited.

'It seemed to be the most important thing when I was growing up. Dad... Mum's life revolved around Dad so she worried about how our behaviour reflected on him, his chances of promotion. After she died it seemed even more important to keep up appearances.'

'So you're worried about what people will say about you?'

'I don't know. Maybe.' She laughed but there was no humour in the sound. 'What does that say about me? A rebel afraid of losing her reputation. Has to be paradox, doesn't it?'

He thought he saw the shimmer of moisture on her eyelashes before she turned her head away from him. 'Kayla. Don't.'

He tugged her into his arms. After a tiny moment of resistance she melted there and feeling her cuddling close felt so right.

'People won't think anything about you and me. Even if they did, I don't give a damn,' he said. 'I don't want some hole-in-the-corner affair with you. If you have any doubts about that, tell me now and I'll take out a full-page ad in the *Dustin Gazette*.'

'Okay.' Her voice was thick.

'Okay, you'll stay the night or I should take out an ad?'

'Okay, I'll stay the night.'

He'd take it. He wanted more, he wanted her to say she'd stay for ever but for now he accepted she was giving him what she could. And it was a damned sight more than he'd expected a few weeks ago.

He could help her, give her room. She was so used to living her life within parameters set by someone else. Rebelling was new to her. For now she needed to feel in control of her plans. He needed to be patient until she was ready to adjust her plans to find a place for him. He could do that.

Tom was like an addiction, Kayla thought. The more she saw of him, the more she wanted to see. She'd missed him during the weekend away on her course, had been impatient to get back to Dustin to see him. It was made worse by the fact that she'd spent every night that week at his place, studying. He'd been great—annoyingly so. When she'd been tempted to play hookey, he'd sat her down at the table and gone out to his workshop so she'd had no excuse to stop studying. Two nights away from him while she'd been down in Melbourne at the course had been awful. It had been his suggestion that she go back to his place on the Sunday night and he'd given her a key to the front door.

He'd made her greedy. She wanted to see as much of him as she could.

She didn't want to think about her plans for now or about the limited time she had in Dustin. Surely the shine on the relationship would have worn off by the time her contract was up. In the meantime, she wanted to revel in the things she was learning about him and about herself.

Surely it wasn't so unreasonable.

CHAPTER FIFTEEN

KAYLA slotted the key into the front door. The pleasant smell of eucalyptus smoke on the frosty air promised warmth inside. Tom had the fire going. Bless him.

A shiver seized her as she entered the foyer and shut the door behind her. Delicious heat curled across her chilled skin. She smiled her pleasure as she stripped off her jacket and hung it on the hallstand. This unprecedented late spring cold snap was brutal, a real taste of winter. Snow flurries had made dazzling white starbursts in the headlights. Beautiful but potentially deadly.

Tom had wanted to travel into town to pick her up after her shift. She'd refused but the gesture had touched her. She wasn't used to such a nurturing approach from men in her life. Having grown up within a rigid set of her father's guidelines, she'd learned not to expect softness, consideration. No cosseting at all.

And here was Tom ready to pamper her as much as she'd let him. His powerful drive to look out for people, for *her*, was as bewildering as it was beguiling.

Her emotions see-sawed back and forth about it. Part of her wanted to bask in his treatment, become accustomed to his brand of spoiling. But another part of her said it would be weak, a step towards losing independence.

She sighed, pushing away the troubling thoughts. For now it was lovely to be home.

Home! *Home?*

She put out a hand to steady herself as the floor seemed to rock beneath her feet. When had she started to think of this as home? This was Tom's place. She didn't belong here. Regardless of how welcome he made her feel.

She took a deep breath and tried to calm the twist in her stomach. When she had steadied, she switched off the front porch light then walked along the hall towards the gentle glow coming from the lounge.

Tom was there, asleep on the sofa. She'd told him not to wait up for her but he had anyway. An open book rested on his chest, rising and falling with each breath.

She tiptoed across to look down at him and her heart squeezed painfully.

He was beautiful in a masculine, angular way. Lean cheeks, square jaw, a strong nose. Dark stubby lashes formed a thick fringe along his closed eyelids. His head had rolled slightly to one side, his mouth relaxed in sleep.

His mouth, so clever and versatile. Firm, commanding lips that demanded a response...soft, teasing lips that seduced a response.

She shivered, not from the cold this time. It was so tempting to bend down, press her mouth to his, taste the tenor of his kisses tonight. He'd make love to her with a generous, tender expertise. The thought made her pulse race. Being with him was spectacular in a way she'd never experienced before.

She would always be glad to have been a part of his life— even for this short interlude. The knowledge that her time here was limited sat in her chest like an unpleasant weight. She pressed her hand to her sternum. Leaving him was going to be harder than she could have predicted. Somehow, over the last couple of weeks, she'd almost ended up living at Tom's place. Perhaps they needed to ease back, see less of each other.

As though he'd read her troubled thoughts, his forehead pleated in a small frown. Perhaps a case at work was bothering him. He was the sort of man others depended on. Responsible, trustworthy. He expected people to bring their problems to him...welcomed it, even. With every last ounce of strength and intelligence, he did whatever he could to help.

He'd have been a good pioneer, resourceful, tough and brave. She smiled at the idea then bent to lift the book off his chest. A second later her wrist was caught by his fingers in a gentle but unbreakable grip.

Her heart leapt into her throat. She snapped her eyes up to meet heavy-lidded eyes so dark they were nearly black.

'Caught you red-handed.' His voice was a sexy, throaty rasp. He took his book from her hand and dropped it carelessly over the arm of the sofa on to the floor. One expert tug and he'd tumbled her into the narrow gap between his body and the cushioning. It was like lying next to a furnace. 'Mmm, now I'm going to have to punish you.'

Still breathless and disorientated from her rapid change of position, she gasped, 'Any excuse.'

'Is that a complaint?' His lips feathered across her temple.

'Only that you're talking too much,' she said, pushing her turmoil further into the back of her mind. She was here now. With him. Winding her arms around his neck, she touched her fingers to his bare nape.

He reared back to grab her hands in his. 'God, woman, your fingers are like blocks of ice.'

'I know.' The warmth of his palms began to seep into her fingers. 'But you're so lovely and warm. I want to snuggle up.'

His weight settled back on her. 'Marry me and you get automatic snuggle rights.'

She froze, the thoughts she'd been having earlier crashing back with a vengeance. 'Tom—'

'All right, you drive a hard bargain.' His mouth closed over hers as he tucked her hands under his jumper. 'You can have snuggle rights anyway.'

All thought of protesting evaporated as his body heat, then his love-making transported her to a place without doubts, filled only with ecstasy.

But much later, in bed, when Tom enfolded her into his warmth, his body spooning against hers beneath the light quilt, her mind returned to her concerns.

'Tom?'

'Mmm-hmm.' His voice rumbled, half-asleep.

'You are happy with the way things are between us, aren't you? You understand it's temporary? I can't stay in Dustin.'

'Mmm.' His hand slipped around her waist, fingers splaying for a moment across her stomach then relaxing as he said, 'I understand what you told me.'

'Okay.' An odd ambivalence shook her. She should be glad... she *was* glad. At least it meant she didn't have to worry about him being hurt...and if she was more involved than she'd anticipated, then that was her problem. Not his. She could let herself have this time to store up memories to sustain her when she moved on. 'Okay. That's good.'

Tom deepened his breathing, relaxed his body consciously. He blinked in the darkness, inhaling Kayla's sweet fragrance. Feeling her body pressed along his, the backs of her thighs aligned with the tops of his, her spine against his stomach and chest. The warmth they created so much more than they'd make individually.

Together they were so much more than they were alone. Couldn't Kayla see that?

He'd hoped time would convince her but tonight he'd rushed. His quip about marriage, the long-term plan, prematurely exposed. The comment had slipped from the deepest recesses of his relaxed mind straight onto his tongue.

Marriage. A wife, a partner to share his life with, to make

a family with. Things he'd promised himself since he'd woken up in the hospital recovery suite after surgery for the gunshot wound. His need had been a slow burn in the last two years... these last few weeks with Kayla had turned it into a raging inferno.

Had he blown his chance with the unguarded words?

She was such a valiant, determined spirit. Driven to prove herself against some standard he couldn't comprehend, she was unnecessarily hard on herself. He was in awe of her already. She had nothing to prove to him. But that was the problem. She had everything to prove to herself. It remained to be seen whether that would mean sacrificing what they had.

He wouldn't let her go easily, be a gentleman about it. He was prepared to bare himself, to let her see his heart and soul.

He'd do whatever it took because he was playing for keeps.

Look out, Kayla, he thought as he tumbled into sleep.

Moments before the alarm went off, Tom felt Kayla slip out of his arms. Still half-asleep, he wondered why she hadn't turned and wrapped her arms around him as she'd got into the habit of doing in the mornings. A heartbeat later, he remembered last night.

Through narrowed eyelids, he watched her leave the room. The shower came on and a short time later he heard her pad down to the kitchen. Stifling a sigh, he rolled over and pushed back the covers.

He had a bad feeling about this morning.

Clean clothes in hand, he headed for the bathroom. The steamy room smelled of her. A combination of soap, shampoo, moisturiser and Kayla. One more part of her presence he'd become used to around the place.

By the time he got to the living area, Kayla was standing in front of the wood heater, a mug in one hand.

'Good morning,' he said, stopping in front of her. He wrapped his fingers around hers and lifted the mug to his lips to take a mouthful of her coffee. 'Mmm, that's good. I love it that you take your coffee the right way.'

Her eyes flickered over his bare torso, a quick flare of interest in the pewter. 'I've got yours ready, I just need to pour it.'

'Thanks.' He grinned and released her.

Kneeling at the hearth, he opened the damper before releasing the catch on the door so he could stoke the fire. A spark landed on his forearm and he brushed it away casually before it could burn.

'You're asking for trouble with all that bare skin,' Kayla said from just behind him.

'I'm trying to impress you with how tough I am.' He stood and took the drink she offered. 'I thought it would improve my chances of getting you back to the bedroom.'

The smile she gave him was tentative, her eyes tinged with sadness to his hypersensitive mind. 'You have a one-track mind.'

'Pretty much.'

Her knuckles gleamed as her fingers tightened around her mug. 'Tom, we need to talk.'

'Uh-oh. The four words a man doesn't want to hear from the woman in his life,' he said, trying to lighten the moment, but she just watched him sombrely. He stroked a finger down her cheek. 'Hon, we've only just got up. What can be so serious at this hour?'

'We are.' Her mouth turned down in a grimace. 'We're serious, Tom. And we said we wouldn't be.'

The temptation to contradict her was strong but it wouldn't be honest so he shrugged. 'So we broke the rules.'

'But it means that I'm not being fair.' She perched on

the edge of one of the armchairs. 'What you said last night made me wonder... You think this is going somewhere, don't you?'

Hell, yes. He settled for a noncommittal 'Well, it might.'

She shook her head. 'It won't, Tom. I'm sorry but it can't. I told you I have plans. I need to see them through. They're important, worthwhile and I need to prove I can do this.'

He crossed to the sofa they'd made love on last night and sat near her, his knees nearly touching hers. 'Who do you need to prove it to, Kayla? Your father? Your ex-fiancé?' He watched tell-tale emotions flicker through her expressive silver eyes. 'You don't have to prove a damned thing to anyone.'

'I have to prove it to me.' Her mouth trembled but her voice was firm.

'Okay.' He dragged a hand down his face, thinking hard, trying to decide a different tack. 'Then what's wrong with plans that allow for some flexibility? Changing a plan isn't a hanging offence. We're good together. Admit it.'

'Tom—'

'We're better than good, we're great.' He clenched his fingers into fists to keep himself from reaching for her.

'Because it's still new, Tom. We're in the honeymoon phase. We're both putting our best foot forward. I'm not staying for the next phase.'

'No pipe and slippers. Message understood.' Blood pounded at his temples.

'You *said* that before.' She stared into her coffee, tension obvious from the set line of her shoulders. 'But now we're getting in too deep and we have to stop.'

'So we'll stop. We won't get in too deep.'

Her haunted grey eyes came back to his. 'No, I mean we need to stop seeing each other now, before we get hurt.'

He rubbed his chest, feeling the pain. She was dumping him. The go-slow plan was out the window...he might as well let her see just how bad he was in.

'You think it's that easy. You've put your cards on the table. Now it's my turn.' He pulled in a deep breath and looked her full in the eye. 'I love you, Kayla Morgan. I would die for you before I would hurt you.'

She looked stricken. Not the look he wanted to see on the face of the woman he'd just bared his soul to. His heart kept beating despite the desperate chill that invaded his chest.

He clenched his jaw, wondering if he had the courage to tell her the rest. But he'd come this far… 'I've let you call the shots in our relationship when all I wanted to do was march you down to the church and tie you up with rings and signatures and legalities.' His throat felt raw. 'This is the lifetime deal for me.'

Begging words paraded through his brain, desperate deals to keep things going. He shut his mouth to stop them from escaping and making him more woeful than he had to be.

'Oh, Tom. I'm so sorry.' She reached out to touch him, her fingers not quite steady.

He twisted away from her. 'That's not a good idea right now, Kayla,' he said. *Pity.* He couldn't bear it. 'Unless you're going to give me something more than sympathy.'

'I—I…' She stopped, unable to say the words he so badly wanted her to say. 'I'm sorry. I can't be what you want.'

'You *are* what I want.' He stood, took several jerky paces away. His frustration at not being able to reach her was like a tightly wound spring needing release. 'Just you being yourself. Nothing more. I'd give anything, do anything, if I could help you to believe that.'

'You make it sound like I need rescuing but I don't, Tom. I know what I have to do.' Kayla looked at Tom's rigid back. Although he hadn't raised his voice, she could hear the tension, the pain, he held in check.

She'd hurt him. The last thing she'd wanted to do. She'd hoped that by being honest with him from the beginning they'd be able to stay heart-whole.

Now she could see how she'd deluded herself. Tom loved her and he'd shown her in so many ways. Because it had suited her, she'd ignored the warning signs. In him. In herself.

They were never supposed to get this serious. How had she let it happen?

She looked at him, at the pain she'd caused, and it was nearly enough to make her buckle. She felt like her heart had been cut out. How she ached to go to him, to offer him whatever it took to make take his pain away.

But she was confused and to weaken would mean hurting him even more.

She was right to end it now. She couldn't steal any more moments from him. He deserved better. He deserved the things he wanted.

Her hand shook as she put aside her half-finished coffee. 'I'll go and get my gear.'

Hardly aware of what she was doing, she went to the bedroom and gathered all her belongings. Tears blinded her as she struggled with the zipper of her carry-all. She stopped, pressed the heels of her hands to her eyes and counted. Control. She had to get herself under control so she could face Tom before going.

She went back to the lounge. He was still standing where she'd left him. He'd looked so shattered. More than anything, she wanted to put her arms around him. But after what she'd done, she had no right to comfort him. And that would only make it worse.

'I'm sorry, Tom. I've made a hash of this. I didn't mean to.'

'I know.' He looked at her, his heart, unashamedly, in his eyes.

She swallowed hard. 'I hope you find what you need.'

'I have.' The small crooked smile he managed tore at her. 'But she doesn't need me.'

'Tom, please…' Her throat threatened to close over.

'What did you expect, Kayla? That I'd make it easy for you?' He shook his head slightly. 'I'm sorry, honey. I'd do a lot of things for you but that's beyond me.'

'Goodbye, Tom.' She turned away quickly, blinking hard as she made her way to the door. Down the steps to her car. Her hands shook so much she had trouble getting the key into the ignition.

She drove carefully, glad of the numbness that allowed her to concentrate on the road. But as soon as she pulled up at her flat, sensation returned with a vengeance. Her heart felt raw, flayed. Her hands clenched on the steering-wheel as sobs erupted from deep within her, racking her until she was exhausted.

Moving like an old, old woman, she collected her bag and let herself into the flat.

She'd made such a mess of things, hurt Tom cruelly when all he'd done had been to treat her well.

He loved her.

She sagged against the door and slid down until she sat on the floor. Fresh tears scalded her eyes.

How could she bear knowing she'd caused him such pain?

CHAPTER SIXTEEN

Tom juggled his handhold on the heavy wardrobe and craned his head around the end of the unit. 'I thought this was supposed to be empty.'

'It is. It's solid cedar,' Liz said.

'I'm starting to think it'd make damned good kindling.' Jack grunted as they manoeuvred the awkward bulk.

'You're nearly there,' Liz said. 'Just a bit further. That's it. Oh, perfect, thank you.' She stood back and beamed, her hands folded over her bulging stomach. Tom looked at her gingerly, wondering exactly when the baby was due.

'Now, will you have a rest, please?' Jack said, sounding close to the end of his tether.

'Okay. As soon as I've made you two a cup of coffee.'

'No. Now. Tom and I will make the coffee. Put your feet up. That's an order.'

'All right, boss.' She and Jack grinned at each other, their faces softening with such overwhelming love that Tom felt like an intruder in the moment. His heart squeezed painfully. This was what he'd wanted with Kayla, what he'd been so sure would be in their future. He'd been wrong.

'Scoot.'

'I'm gone.' She grinned.

Jack frowned at the empty doorway after Liz had left the

room. 'Not planning to take Kayla far afield tonight, are you, mate?'

'Not tonight,' Tom said. *Not any night for the foreseeable future.* The agony of it battered him. He clamped his jaw. 'Why?'

His friend rolled his shoulders as though to release the tension there. 'Liz is in the first stages of labour.'

'What? Now?' Aghast, Tom stared at his friend. 'Shouldn't you do something? Boil water? Go to the hospital?'

'If I had my way, she'd be chained to a hospital bed right now,' Jack muttered, then shrugged. 'She says it's too early. Come on, let's make that coffee.'

Tom followed him into the kitchen.

A split second later, Liz appeared, an odd look on her face and her hands clutching her stomach. 'Change of plans, darling.'

Jack was beside her in a flash. 'Now? Is it now?'

'Yes. Time to go to the hospital.'

'I'll drive. We'll take my car,' Tom said, digging his keys out of his pocket as Jack scooped Liz into his arms. 'It's in the driveway ready to go.'

'Wait,' she said, as Jack strode towards the door. 'I need to ring Kayla and I want my bag.'

'We can ring on the way,' Jack said. 'I'll come back for your bag later.'

'No. I want it now. There's no need to panic. I'm not going to drop your son on the front veranda,' Liz said. 'Please, darling.'

'I'll ring Kayla while you get the bag, Jack,' Tom said, picking up the handset on the bench and punching in Kayla's number.

'Hell. All right.' Jack lowered Liz gently onto a chair. 'Stay,' he said, then stalked out of the room.

'Hey, Liz, sweetie.' Kayla's husky voice, warm, loving and calm, flowed down the phone line like honey and Tom's pulse leapt painfully. 'I've been expecting your call. Are you ready to come in?'

His unruly heart clamoured regardless of the fact that all her sweet reassurance wasn't meant for him.

'Kayla, it's Tom,' he rasped.

'Tom?' There was a fraction of a second of stark silence on the other end of the line. He could almost feel her shock, hear her thoughts spinning, but before he could reassure her, she said, 'Is Liz all right?'

'She's in labour. Jack's just getting her bag and then we'll be on our way.'

'Okay. Ask Liz what stage.' Her voice was steady, unhurried. 'Have her waters broken?'

'Kayla wants to know what stage you're at and if your waters have broken.'

'My waters haven't broken and the contractions—' Liz stopped abruptly, her face screwed up as she puffed. 'Two minutes apart and getting stronger. Near transition.'

It was all he could do to subdue the dismay that mushroomed through him. They'd done the theory of delivering babies but he'd never imagined having to use the rusty knowledge. He relayed Liz's information. 'She says she's not far off transition, whatever that means.'

'It means don't panic but don't dawdle either.' He could hear the smile in Kayla's voice. It curled into his ears like a caress. She was strong and calm on the other end of the line, instilling her confidence over the phone. Not that Liz needed it. But he did. 'Tell Liz the room is all ready and I'll see her soon. Drive carefully, Tom.'

'I will.' He thumbed the off button as Jack came back into the room. 'Okay, give me the bag, you get Liz. Let's go.'

Tom curbed his impatience on the short drive to the hospital. He was torn between wanting to floor it with emergency lights blazing, sirens blaring, and wanting to make the ride as smooth as possible for his precious cargo.

Most of all, he wanted to be *there*, with Kayla and her expertise.

As he drove, he listened to his friend's murmurs of reassurance coming from the back seat.

At the emergency entrance, he could see Kayla at the door with a wheelchair. He felt his tension leach away, only to be replaced by the profound sadness he'd lived with for the last week. Despite the grinding physical ache that cramped in his chest, he couldn't take his eyes off Kayla. She looked beautiful, perhaps a little pale.

'I want to walk,' Liz insisted as she clambered out of back door. 'I need to walk. Jack?'

'Right here, darling.'

'Let's get you set up in the birthing room.' Kayla ushered them through the door, looking back at him with a sweet smile. 'Thanks, Tom. You did good.'

The quick words of gratitude, the way her beautiful grey eyes had clung to his with soft warmth and approval, filled him with an odd painful pleasure.

The door shut behind them. He'd done his bit, he could go home now...should go home.

But he didn't want to. There was nothing, *no one*, waiting for him there. Seeing Kayla tonight underlined the emptiness he felt.

He sighed and climbed into the driver's seat. Perhaps he'd park the vehicle, stay a bit longer in case Jack and Liz needed him.

Less than an hour later, Kayla smiled at her friends huddled together, their new baby boy cradled lovingly.

'I'll leave you three alone to get acquainted. If you need anything at all, the buzzer's there. Just ring.'

Jack and Liz looked up, their eyes damp. 'Thanks, Kayla.'

'Thank you for letting me be here.' She smiled through the tears brimming in her eyes. 'All of you did a great job.'

Turning away, she let herself out of the room quietly. Her heart was so full. The miracle of birth was always profound, but today it had affected her even more than usual.

She stood with her fingertips resting on the wood of the closed door. In a moment of crystal clarity she realised this was what she wanted. A future with a man she loved, with Tom. He'd offered her a place in his heart and she'd been too afraid to grasp it.

But now she knew what she had to do. Urgency gripped her and she hoped against hope that Tom would still be in the waiting room. Not taking the time to change out of her scrubs, she hurried along the corridor. She'd made a mistake and it was time to face it, own it. And make what amends she could.

The damage she'd done might be irrevocable but, regardless, she had to tell Tom how she felt. She had to put her heart on the line and take a risk.

Tom loved her...or at least he *had* loved her. She needed to ask if he'd give her a second chance.

Her footsteps slowed as she scanned the room of patients waiting to be attended to. Tom wasn't there. Disappointment punctured her, leaving a brutal, unhappy void in her stomach. She'd pinned so much on being about to see him straight away.

'Are you looking for Tom?' Hilda asked from behind the desk.

'Yes.' Kayla felt her chin tremble as she looked at the kindly nurse. 'Is he still around?'

'He's only just walked out.' Hilda nodded towards the door. 'You can probably still catch him if you hurry.'

'Thanks.'

As soon as she was out of the door, Kayla broke into a run towards Tom's four-wheel drive.

Eyes closed, he was sitting behind the steering-wheel. She

knocked on the glass of the driver's window. His eyes flew open then widened when he saw her.

The window was down in a trice and he barked at her, 'Jack and Liz?'

'They're fine. Fine. All three of them.'

He seemed to sag. 'Thank God.'

'I'm sorry. I didn't mean to scare you like that.' Now that she'd tracked him down she felt oddly tongue tied. She put her hands on the doorframe, wrapping her fingers over the edge of the open window. 'Tom, I… Can we go somewhere to talk?'

A muscle along his jaw flexed and she read rejection in his eyes. Pain tightened her chest.

'Kayla—'

'Please,' she whispered, gripping harder and willing him to hear her out.

He sighed out a breath. 'Okay. I'm listening.'

She hesitated then swallowed. 'Can I…can I get in?'

'Of course.'

She walked around to the other side of the vehicle as she tried to gather her thoughts. Suddenly Tom was beside her, opening the door.

She turned to face him, looked up into his dear, dear face. Suddenly his features blurred and she blinked hard to bring him back into focus.

'I'm sorry for hurting you the way I did, Tom.'

'I know. It's not your fault. You tried to warn me.' A sad smile touched his lips. 'I just didn't want to hear because I was so busy with my own plans.'

He was trying to make it better, easier for her. He was baring himself again and it was her job. A hot tear streaked down her face.

'Stop. Please.' She laid her fingertips to his mouth. 'I'm doing this all wrong.'

He lifted a hand and stroked the moisture from her cheek.

Covering his hand with hers, she turned her head and placed
a kiss in the palm.

'Kayla—'

'I love you, Tom.' She felt a jolt run through his body as
the words rasped in her throat. She'd said them, they were
out there. It was as if a huge weight had been lifted from her
soul. Saying the rest would be easy now. 'I want to be with
you. I'm sorry I hurt you and I know you might have changed
your mind.'

'Changed my mind? Are you crazy? Not in a million years.
I love you so much it hurts.' He freed his hands and she found
herself crushed to his body. 'God. Say the words again so I
know I didn't imagine them.'

'I love you, Tom.'

He squeezed her hard and she revelled in the embrace.
Tremors shook them. Did they come from him or her? It didn't
matter. All that mattered was they were together.

His lips found hers. She dived into the kiss, not holding
back any part of herself, relishing how much sweeter and even
more perfect the feel of his mouth on hers was now that her
emotions were stripped naked.

He pulled back, brushing her hair back and looking deep
into her eyes. 'Your plans. What about your plans, Kayla?
Honey, you're so passionate about them.'

'A reason to avoid life and pain and messy emotions and
the scary out-of-control way you make me feel. I don't want
to avoid that any more. I still want to make plans but I want
to make them with you.'

'I've got some plans of my own.' He pressed her back
against the fender of the vehicle.

She laughed. 'I already know what one of them is.'

'Yeah.' Colour flared along his cheekbones. 'Well, we'll
get to that. But we've got some more important things to settle
first…make an honest man of me.'

'As soon as you like.'

'Family?'

'Oh, yes. I can't wait until we start working on that plan. I love you, Tom. Take me home.'

MAY 2011
HARDBACK TITLES

ROMANCE

Too Proud to be Bought	Sharon Kendrick
A Dark Sicilian Secret	Jane Porter
Prince of Scandal	Annie West
The Beautiful Widow	Helen Brooks
Strangers in the Desert	Lynn Raye Harris
The Ultimate Risk	Chantelle Shaw
Sins of the Past	Elizabeth Power
A Night With Consequences	Margaret Mayo
Cupcakes and Killer Heels	Heidi Rice
Sex, Gossip and Rock & Roll	Nicola Marsh
Riches to Rags Bride	Myrna Mackenzie
Rancher's Twins: Mum Needed	Barbara Hannay
The Baby Project	Susan Meier
Second Chance Baby	Susan Meier
The Love Lottery	Shirley Jump
Her Moment in the Spotlight	Nina Harrington
Her Little Secret	Carol Marinelli
The Doctor's Damsel in Distress	Janice Lynn

HISTORICAL

Lady Drusilla's Road to Ruin	Christine Merrill
Glory and the Rake	Deborah Simmons
To Marry a Matchmaker	Michelle Styles
The Mercenary's Bride	Terri Brisbin

MEDICAL™

The Taming of Dr Alex Draycott	Joanna Neil
The Man Behind the Badge	Sharon Archer
St Piran's: Tiny Miracle Twins	Maggie Kingsley
Maverick in the ER	Jessica Matthews

MAY 2011
LARGE PRINT TITLES

ROMANCE

Hidden Mistress, Public Wife	Emma Darcy
Jordan St Claire: Dark and Dangerous	Carole Mortimer
The Forbidden Innocent	Sharon Kendrick
Bound to the Greek	Kate Hewitt
Wealthy Australian, Secret Son	Margaret Way
A Winter Proposal	Lucy Gordon
His Diamond Bride	Lucy Gordon
Juggling Briefcase & Baby	Jessica Hart

HISTORICAL

Courting Miss Vallois	Gail Whitiker
Reprobate Lord, Runaway Lady	Isabelle Goddard
The Bride Wore Scandal	Helen Dickson
Chivalrous Captain, Rebel Mistress	Diane Gaston

MEDICAL™

Dr Zinetti's Snowkissed Bride	Sarah Morgan
The Christmas Baby Bump	Lynne Marshall
Christmas in Bluebell Cove	Abigail Gordon
The Village Nurse's Happy-Ever-After	Abigail Gordon
The Most Magical Gift of All	Fiona Lowe
Christmas Miracle: A Family	Dianne Drake

**JUNE 2011
HARDBACK TITLES**

ROMANCE

Passion and the Prince	Penny Jordan
For Duty's Sake	Lucy Monroe
Alessandro's Prize	Helen Bianchin
Mr and Mischief	Kate Hewitt
Wife in the Shadows	Sara Craven
The Brooding Stranger	Maggie Cox
An Inconvenient Obsession	Natasha Tate
The Girl He Never Noticed	Lindsay Armstrong
The Privileged and the Damned	Kimberly Lang
The Big Bad Boss	Susan Stephens
Her Desert Prince	Rebecca Winters
A Family for the Rugged Rancher	Donna Alward
The Boss's Surprise Son	Teresa Carpenter
Soldier on Her Doorstep	Soraya Lane
Ordinary Girl in a Tiara	Jessica Hart
Tempted by Trouble	Liz Fielding
Flirting with the Society Doctor	Janice Lynn
When One Night Isn't Enough	Wendy S Marcus

HISTORICAL

Ravished by the Rake	Louise Allen
The Rake of Hollowhurst Castle	Elizabeth Beacon
Bought for the Harem	Anne Herries
Slave Princess	Juliet Landon

MEDICAL™

Melting the Argentine Doctor's Heart	Meredith Webber
Small Town Marriage Miracle	Jennifer Taylor
St Piran's: Prince on the Children's Ward	Sarah Morgan
Harry St Clair: Rogue or Doctor?	Fiona McArthur

JUNE 2011
LARGE PRINT TITLES

ROMANCE

Flora's Defiance	Lynne Graham
The Reluctant Duke	Carole Mortimer
The Wedding Charade	Melanie Milburne
The Devil Wears Kolovsky	Carol Marinelli
The Nanny and the CEO	Rebecca Winters
Friends to Forever	Nikki Logan
Three Weddings and a Baby	Fiona Harper
The Last Summer of Being Single	Nina Harrington

HISTORICAL

Lady Arabella's Scandalous Marriage	Carole Mortimer
Dangerous Lord, Seductive Miss	Mary Brendan
Bound to the Barbarian	Carol Townend
The Shy Duchess	Amanda McCabe

MEDICAL™

St Piran's: The Wedding of The Year	Caroline Anderson
St Piran's: Rescuing Pregnant Cinderella	Carol Marinelli
A Christmas Knight	Kate Hardy
The Nurse Who Saved Christmas	Janice Lynn
The Midwife's Christmas Miracle	Jennifer Taylor
The Doctor's Society Sweetheart	Lucy Clark